CORNER Boys

Robert Hunt

CORNER Boys

ROBERT HUNT

FLANKER PRESS LIMITED
ST. JOHN'S

Library and Archives Canada Cataloguing in Publication

Hunt, Robert J., 1949-
Corner boys / Robert Hunt.

Also issued in electronic format.
ISBN 978-1-926881-50-8

1. Hunt, Robert J., 1949- --Childhood and youth. 2. St. John's (N.L.)--Biography. I. Title.

FC2196.26.H85A3 2011 971.8'104092 C2011-906109-0

PRINTED IN CANADA

Cover Design: Peter Hanes
Edited by Susan Rendell

FLANKER PRESS
PO BOX 2522, STATION C
ST. JOHN'S, NL, CANADA
TOLL FREE: 1-866-739-4420
WWW.FLANKERPRESS.COM

15 14 13 12 11 1 2 3 4 5 6 7 8 9

Canada

Canada Council for the Arts Conseil des Arts du Canada

Newfoundland Labrador

We acknowledge the financial support of the Government of Canada through the Book Publishing Industry Development Program (BPIDP) for our publishing activities; the Canada Council for the Arts which last year invested $20.1 million in writing and publishing throughout Canada; the Government of Newfoundland and Labrador, Department of Tourism, Culture and Recreation.

This book is dedicated to my good friend and co-author of three books, Lisa J. Ivany of Gander. I will always remember how we first met, through 9/11, and how we penned our first book, *Christmas Memories*, together. Many thanks to Lisa for the kindness that she and her mom, Maggie, and the rest of her family have shown me over the years. This book is for you, Lisa, for your friendship and inspiration.

This book is also dedicated to my best childhood friend, Malcolm "Dickie" White. I will never forget the times we spent together in the 1950s, 1960s, and 1970s in St. John's. Those days will live forever in my mind and in my heart.

contents

preface

On December 28, 2006, I received a phone call from my oldest brother, Edward, informing me that Malcolm "Dickie" White had passed away earlier that day. Edward told me that Dickie had been staying at his mother's house for Christmas, and had gone to bed the night before complaining that he wasn't feeling well. He got out of bed the next morning and dropped dead. A massive heart attack. The paramedics administered CPR, but to no avail. He was gone, and with him went part of my soul.

My brother sounded sad. I was in shock. Dickie was one of the original "corner boys." In the years that we were friends, he was more than a good buddy. He was my mentor, bodyguard, and hero. I adored him and his approach to life. Absolutely nothing bothered him. In all the years I knew him, I only once saw him angry. He was the most gentle man I ever knew.

He was a special man. He did what he wanted to do, not what others wanted him to do. No one ever said anything bad about him. Everybody loved him. I think God was short an angel in heaven that day, and decided that Malcolm "Dickie" White was just what He was looking for.

I was a year older than Dickie, but he was years wiser. What initially attracted me to him was that he was a very quiet and shy person who rarely got excited. (Unlike me: one of Dickie's jobs was to keep me on an even keel.) He always had an unassuming look, a sort of I-know-what-you're-thinking expression. He was never really happy, never really sad. He was a favourite among his friends and well-liked by his peers. Everyone trusted him.

I was always proud to be able to call him my friend. The more I was with him over the years, the greater the respect I had for him.

****

Edward has always said, "Enjoy your life now, for you could wake up dead tomorrow." I use these words a lot. Time stops for no man, and those irreplaceable days of the past went by far too quickly. Some of those cherished days will be inside the hearts of my friends and me until the day we leave this earth. I know the ones I remember will. We all have memories, and sometimes our thoughts creep back into the past they come from. When we meet an old friend from the neighbourhood, or when we hear someone speak of a time, place, or person from long ago that we had forgotten about. Or when someone we grew up with dies.

To me, those days, those months, those years were a beautiful lesson in how life should be lived. And, boy, did my friends and I ever enjoy living it!

Back then, it was a place where you left the doors of your home open and your car doors unlocked, and where children were seen and not heard. It was a time when people were polite, and they cared for one another. You had respect for older people, and called your father "sir" and your mother "ma'am." You opened a door for a lady. You carried an older person's groceries home when they had a long walk from the corner store. They were times when we cared for elderly people, and had a healthy fear of behaving disrespectfully toward authority. Oh my, how times have changed!

young years

I was born on February 23, 1949, at St. Clare's Hospital in St. John's, a little more than a month before the province of Newfoundland and Labrador joined Canada. This makes me a true Newfoundlander. I was the second of five children, all sons: Edward, Robert, Calvin, Hubert, and the youngest of the lot, Angus. God didn't bless Mom and Dad with a daughter.

I lived at 36 McKay Street for the first six years of my life, but my memory is vague when it comes to those years. The house we lived in had two storeys, and someone else lived in the upstairs part. I think it was an elderly lady. Mom was always going upstairs to check on whoever lived there, anyway. The four or five steps leading to the front door were concrete. The house had a big front window that Ed and I used to look out before we went to bed, staring at the stars and dreaming far-off, boyish dreams.

I do remember sleighing, one incident in particular. A bunch of kids, including me, were sliding down Leslie or Richmond Street, and going under an oil truck that was making a delivery in the process. I had a small sleigh made of wooden slats with steel runners, and it got jammed under the truck. I would have been run over or dragged off by the truck if a woman hadn't spotted me and alerted the driver before he got back in and drove off. The driver took me home, and Mom and Dad gave me hell for my escapade.

I also remember going to St. Clare's on a stormy winter day to have my tonsils removed at the tender age of five. My dad sat next to my mother in the back seat of a large car and held me in his arms all the way to the hospital. It was snowing hard and the roads were slippery. Whose car it was will always remain a mystery: Dad couldn't drive, and there weren't many vehicles in St. John's in those days.

Years later, I met a girl on McKay Street who became my first steady girlfriend. Her name was Rita Powell, and what a beauty she was.

Even though I was only six, the family's move from McKay Street to Brazil Street in 1955 shattered my little world. Dad told us many years later that we were supposed to live on Brazil Street for only a little while. He had intended to find another house in the city, he said. We ended up staying on Brazil for twenty-one years. Later in life I realized that Dad couldn't afford to buy a better house, and I think that leaving McKay Street for Brazil bothered him (although he never said anything, being a proud man). McKay was considered a better neighbourhood, and CN workers such as my father tended to live in the west end, on streets such as McKay and Craigmillar. (The Reid Newfoundland Company, which built the Newfoundland railway, gave mortgages to its employees to build houses on the south side of Craigmillar. These houses, which are still in existence, were known as Railway Range.) But once we settled in on Brazil and he met some neighbours, Dad seemed to be at ease with the move.

the centre of the city

It was on Brazil Street that I met Dickie White, who was to become my best and closest friend, and who would lead me from the age of innocence into the age of mischief. (Of course, even at six, I was no angel myself.) I remember my first meeting with Dickie White well. It was in June of 1955, the day we moved to Brazil Street.

It was a fine June day, and Dickie and his younger sister, Louise, were sitting on the front steps of 38 Brazil Street, the house next to ours (which was number 40). Neither of them said a word to us as we settled in. They just kept staring at us as if we were intruders.

Dickie's stare scared the living crap out of me. He just had *that* look. Also, he was big, and that intimidated me. (I soon became very happy that he was my friend and not my enemy.) And then he came into our house and sat down as if he were part of the family. Mom and Dad took to him right away, and he ended up becoming an honorary Hunt for many years.

It only took a small part of the day to move in. Our

family didn't own much. We didn't have a lot of furniture. Mom and Dad came home a few days later with more. We were now living in the poor section of town.

After we finished stowing things away, I sat on the front steps. Dickie approached me, speaking in his quiet, steady tone. He was about a foot taller than me and weighed around ninety or a hundred pounds. But it turned out that he was as pleasant as a sleeping dog. Unless he got angry, which was rare. Whoever got him mad was in big trouble.

(When he got older most people backed off after one look at him, saying, "Yes, sir." I know I did.)

"Want to have some fun?" Dickie said.

I was hooked. "Why not?" I said. And that was the start of a wonderful friendship.

****

The first place we visited was "the corner," where we would trade stories and secrets for the next twenty years. The corner was situated at the bottom of Brazil and Casey Streets, and extended over to Central Street. It was Y-shaped and extended halfway out into Casey Street. There were no trees. There was no sidewalk, either. Cars always seemed to zoom by at breakneck speeds, and we had to be very careful when we stepped away from the store or the houses. Only three or four feet separated the houses from the road.

There was a store, which was the focal point of the corner. The steps to the store were curved, and the door was on the corner. It had two large windows, one on the Casey/Central Street store side, and another on the

Brazil Street side. At the end of the store on the Central Street side were three steps that led to the Taylors' (the family who lived above the store). Next to the store on that side were the Kings, in an old three-storey house (Jimmy King and his older brother Edward would become good friends). On the Brazil Street side of the store lived Kay Hann, a sweetheart of a lady who was always good to us when we were young boys. Next to Kay's was Dickie's house, and next to Dickie's, of course, was our house. The corner is long gone, but both our houses are still there. (In fact, Dickie's mother, who is in her eighties now, is still there; I drop in and have a chat with her from time to time.)

The store was owned by three different people when we were growing up. The first owner was Kevin King. Many years later it was owned by Frank "Fossie" Furlong, a great dart player who competed in many of the city's dart tournaments. The last owners I remember were Bette Royal and her husband "Socks" Phelan, from Casey Street. Bette's brother Pat was a long-time sports fan and a great contributor to sports, especially baseball and softball.

The corner, and later our clubhouse, would be our main hangouts. In those days we didn't know what boredom was. We never had time to get bored.

Back then, the centre of St. John's was different from any other area of the city. It was the hub of downtown. All the real action took place on Water Street, the busiest section of the city, which was only a stone's throw from our homes. Dickie took me everywhere, showing me the new neighbourhood, all the hiding spots and interesting places. I was in awe: I had never been out of my own neighbourhood of McKay Street, although I had heard about other parts of town from school friends. I had never even been to Water Street—it was too far away from McKay for me to be allowed to walk there at my age—but I had envisioned it many times in my mind.

The area in which I now lived, just up from Water Street and New Gower Street, was the heart of the city: its bustling crowds and loud noises were new experiences for me. It was very exciting to explore the streets I had heard so much about. Before the days of malls, Water Street was the main shopping district for all of Newfoundland. People from the surrounding areas of the city, and indeed from all over the island, went to Water Street to take care of their families' needs. My aunts and uncles came in from around the bay once or twice during the year. Before they made the trip, Mom and Dad would send them stuff cut out of magazines, and catalogues from Bowring's, Woolworths, and other stores on Water Street, especially before Christmas. Bowring's had their Christmas catalogue out at the end of October, as did Woolworths and other stores. If you couldn't get in to town, you ordered from the catalogues and your goods were shipped by train or coastal boat.

Not too many people owned a car in those days; most people walked wherever they needed to go. Everyone walked from all corners of the city to shop on the oldest street in North America. Everything new was to be found on Water Street, until the Avalon Mall came along in the late 1960s.

Water Street was always crowded in its heyday,

especially during Christmas, when it was decorated to the max. The Water Street merchants made a fortune when Christmas came around. As a boy, I loved the charity raffles that took place during the Christmas season.

The Mount Cashel Raffle was the main one. Our family always went there. It was in support of the boys at the Roman Catholic Church's Mount Cashel, an orphanage for boys. The Mount Cashel Raffle was held in a building on Water Street near the lower end of George Street. It usually started during the first week in December and ended on Christmas Eve. It was a big event, and there was always a crowd. The boys of Mount Cashel sold the tickets, supervised by members of the Irish Christian Brothers (the order that founded Mount Cashel). Tickets were usually three for five cents, and a spin of the big wheel determined the winner. Certain draws resulted in cash prizes ranging from $1 to $3. Others were for boxes of cookies or chocolates, coats, shirts, slacks, games, or toys. Businesses all over St. John's donated the prizes. Turkeys, strutting around in the window, were also drawn for, and to win one was a real treat because they cost a lot of money. It was very hard for us kids to get tickets while a spin was on the go because the grown-ups would muscle us out of the way.

The orphanage would eventually become the centre of a sexual abuse scandal that shocked Newfoundland and the world. But I wasn't a bit surprised. I knew some of the Christian Brothers who were convicted—they taught in Catholic schools throughout the city. I always felt in my heart that there was something wrong with the way they behaved toward us. Some of the Brothers were powder kegs waiting to explode.

Many of the stores on the Water Street of my day now exist only in memory. There was Parker and Monroe's shoe store, which sold shoes of "all shapes and sizes," as their window sign said. Variety stores like The Big Six, and The Arcade, owned by former St. John's Mayor John Murphy. Templeton's paint shop was a downtown fixture and it still is. Dickie and I delivered paint for Templeton's on foot for years to different areas of St. John's, before they bought a delivery van, around 1960. Ayre & Sons was a big, family-owned store in the heart of Water Street.

Bowring Brothers was another one, providing shoppers with every modern item, things that couldn't be found anywhere else in Newfoundland. The store had two levels, with two sets of stairs. Bowring's was always trying to outdo Woolworths with respect to pricing. It was the first business in St. John's to have parking on top of the building. Bowring's served some of the best food, bar none, that one could ever eat in St. John's. Mrs. Jean Abbott from Conception Bay South ran Bowring's restaurant, the Captain's Cabin, for many years. It had a fantastic view of the harbour and was considered a fancy restaurant, but the prices weren't high. Everyone went there. Their hot turkey and hot roast beef sandwiches were second to none in St. John's. A specialty was pork chops; no one made pork chops like they did. The desserts were beyond compare; I particularly remember their butterscotch pudding and cobbler pie.

I remember when the London, New York and Paris,

another landmark store, first opened its doors. The building it was in was constructed after the fire of 1892, and first housed James Baird, a fishery supply and general import business. My mother shopped at the London many times over the years. Money was always in short supply, of course, so Mom was always very thrifty, as mothers were in those days. She bought shirts, shorts, underwear, socks, etc., at the London and the Arcade because they had better bargains than most of the stores on Water Street. I seemed to be always trying on clothes at both stores when I was with Mom. My brothers and I were all about the same size, so I got to be the family mannequin—she would get me to try things on, and gauge whether they would fit my brothers. But I didn't mind: I knew there would be a treat at the end of it. We usually ended up at Marty's Restaurant for a snack so she could rest before the walk home to Brazil Street.

At its height, Woolworths, which opened in the early '60s, was the most modern store of its kind in the province. It had some of the first escalators in Newfoundland, and also one of the first PA systems; you heard the latest hits by the top artists—Elvis Presley, Neil Diamond, Roy Orbison, Peggy Lee, Tammy Wynette, The Beatles, The Rolling Stones, The Dave Clarke Five—while you shopped.

Of course, the very top band of the day was The Beatles. I worked at Woolworths part-time during my school years, and I used to ask the person on the third floor who controlled the music to play their songs over and over. Beatlemania arrived in Newfoundland in 1963. The Beatles' music was everywhere. Around the same time, a song called "The Monster Mash," by Bobby "Boris" Pickett, made it really big—it was the most popular song on the airwaves and in the store for a full summer.

As a young child, it was a special thing to go shopping with my mom or dad in the evenings. When my brothers and I tagged along downtown, we knew that we would receive a treat. Of course, we had to tag along with our parents anyway, to help bring home the packages. Dad always made us go with Mom while he was working, because of her heart condition. She wasn't allowed to go anywhere alone, especially to Water Street, because she wasn't able to carry parcels up the steep hill of Casey Street on the way back to the house.

For me and my friends, Water Street was not only a place to shop, it was somewhere we could earn money. I worked part-time at Woolworths from 1963 to 1965, and I have many fond memories of manning the candy counter. In the first six months of that particular stint, I gained about ten pounds, since I frequently sampled the merchandise.

My boss at the time was a rather unsavoury person named Mr. Church. He was a smart business person, but very mean when it came to the customers. One woman used to frequent the store regularly with her three kids, and she always came to the candy counter. I would always add a few extra candies to the bag, because she couldn't afford to spend much money on her children. At least I did until Mr. Church found out and put a stop to it. No money, no freebies. But I found a way around that: I slipped the extra candy into her shopping bag when he wasn't around. To hell with Mr. Church and his rules!

Dickie and I made deliveries for The Big Six. We received a dime or a quarter, depending on how far we had to walk to deliver the merchandise. We always had to bring back a note signed by the customer indicating that they had received the goods. After we showed the note, we could collect our delivery fee; this was the store's way of making sure we hadn't ripped them off. We also shovelled snow for The London, New York and Paris, The Big Six, Woolworths, and smaller stores. It would take us two to three hours to clear the sidewalk in front of Woolworths, which was 150 feet long and ten feet wide. The Arcade was next to Woolworths, and its sidewalk was about twenty feet long. Next door to The Arcade was The Big Six, which had a sidewalk approximately the same size as The Arcade's. The London's was between sixty and seventy feet long. We had no set price for this work and considered ourselves lucky to make a couple of dollars. Money in one's pocket was a rare thing in those days.

We considered ourselves especially lucky when Woolworths hired us to shovel snow. Usually we were treated to a free meal in their restaurant and given $2. We were grateful for the food and the money; there were few ways for young boys to make a couple of shekels in those days, and we could never have afforded anything on the menu. We were always hungry.

When you needed shoes in St. John's in those days, you went to Parker and Monroe's on Water Street. They had every shoe imaginable, and they always stocked shoes that were the shoe "craze" at any particular time.

Everyone—men, women, and children—wore John Whites back then. John White's were British Oxford-style shoes, and they were tough but comfortable. You could have a pair of John Whites for about six years before they started to wear out, and then you passed them down to a younger brother or sister, and he or she probably got another year or two out of them. When our John White's did start to wear, we took them to Jack Kidney's shoe repair on Brazil Square, and he would put new soles and heels on them. If I am not mistaken, Parker and Monroe sold the first Beatle boots, which were a craze in the early '60s. I bought my first pair of loafers, which is something our family could never afford, when I worked for Woolworths.

If you wanted good value but didn't have much money, The Arcade was the place to shop. The owner, John Murphy (former mayor of St. John's), was always there to help and to talk to the customers. He was a very friendly, easygoing man. I went there often with my mom. One day she wanted wallpaper for our bedrooms, but she didn't have enough money for the amount of wallpaper she needed. A salesman asked her where her husband worked. When she said "CN," he let her have the wallpaper on credit. Try that today! In those days, your word was your bond, and people trusted one another.

Another store we frequented was Bon Marche. It sold the same kinds of things as The Arcade, but of a lesser quality.

Sadly, all these stores, except Templeton's, have now passed into history.

****

Between the ages of eight and fourteen, Dickie and I did odd jobs on Water Street, making whatever money we could. In those days, we could walk Water Street blindfolded: we knew every nook and cranny of it. Besides doing errands for the stores, we were always at Job's, Steers, or Baird's Cove when the fishermen brought in their catch. I remember fishermen selling codfish that weighed as much as twenty pounds for only a couple of dollars. The fish was sold rolled up in newspapers. Fish was plentiful in those days, and there was always a steady stream of people going to Water Street to buy it. It was a main source of cheap food.

We would help the men unload their catch, and they would give us the tongues from the cod to sell. We sold them by the bagful for a bit of pocket change. We sometimes delivered fish for a few pennies; the fishermen knew they could trust us not to steal it, or the money we got when we delivered it. Dickie's father, Harold "Blackie" White, was a fisherman, and he always gave us a few fish to deliver around the city.

Back then, most of us growing up in the downtown area of St. John's were poor. Our parents had a rough time making ends meet, so we had to be resourceful if we wanted any extra money to buy some of the things middle-class kids had. Men worked outside the home, generally, so the entire household depended on one small salary. Some women made money from cleaning or sewing or baking for the better-off classes.

If Dickie and I couldn't earn what we needed, we sometimes resorted to other methods. An old friend of mine, Doug Grouchy, had a method of getting a free meal at Woolworths. Doug could do it only when there was a waitress working who hadn't been hoodwinked by him in the past.

I didn't know anything about Doug's game until one day when I was sitting with him in a booth in the restaurant at Woolworths, and Doug ordered a feast of a meal. I wondered how he was going to pay for it, but I plowed in anyway. Anything that was free, you ate! Then we had dessert, and I was really getting worried about how he was going to foot the bill. But good old Doug remained cool and calm. Finally, I asked him how he was paying for the enormous amount of food we had eaten. He told me he didn't have the money, but not to worry. We sat there until the waitress went off her shift, and then Doug went to the counter and ordered two glasses of Coke from the new waitress. I was sweating like a bull.

Doug pocketed the bill, which was on the counter, for the meal we had just finished, and casually walked back to the booth. We moved to a table. When we finished the Cokes, he went back to the counter and paid for them. We then left the building post-haste. We pulled that little trick about once every two months.

Another main source of income was delivering *The Daily News*, a local newspaper whose offices were on Duckworth Street. Dickie and I made a few extra cents on the side with the newspapers. While we were selling them to customers in the Water and Gower Street areas, we sometimes "borrowed" a few papers when no one was looking, sold them, and kept the money. We figured it wasn't dishonest unless you got caught, and we rarely were.

For a long time, there used to be a police officer

directing traffic on the intersection of Prescott and Duckworth streets. It was considered a dangerous place for traffic. Some of the police officers who patrolled P and D were Mel Parsons, Alan Tilley, Don Harris, Frank Miller, George Sheppard, and Fred Windsor. Dickie and I used to try to run across the street behind their backs. We enjoyed the thrill of disobeying authority, even if it was in a small way. When we got caught, which happened a few times, we were severely scolded, which served us right. We could have been struck by a car or truck.

When I go down to Water Street these days, I always think of the Portuguese fishermen of the White Fleet who used to play soccer on the waterfront. We had many games with them, and, *man*, could some of them ever play. We would go down there as a team and lose to them about ninety per cent of the time. We figured any one of those talented men could have been Olympic contenders. They were always good about it, and they treated us well. After every game, they shook hands with each other and with us. And although they were only poor fishermen—their boats were shabby and they, like us, seemed to live on a diet of mostly fish—they always gave us something to eat after the game, and they would let us board the ships and look around. We loved it when they came into port! Everyone did: people used to bring them second-hand clothes and food.

brazil street

In the 1960s and 1970s, Brazil Street was made up of low-rent or low-mortgage housing, where many hard-working people such as my dad lived with their families. There were also people who couldn't find work and had no choice but to live on welfare. Here we survived—and flourished.

Brazil Street is in the centre of St. John's. It intersects Casey Street at its lower end; Monroe Street is in the middle and Lemarchant Road runs across its top. At the top of Brazil Street there was an open meadow called Caul's Field. We used to play softball there and throw parties. It is now the site of Cabot Street Apartments.

Tooton's Photography was across the street from Caul's Field, on Cabot Street. Originally known as the Parisian Photographic Studio, Tooton's was founded in 1905 by Anthony Tooton, a native of Syria who had studied photography in Paris before immigrating to St. John's. The Tooton house and the main business were on this site; the flagship store was on Water Street. A family-run business for three generations, Tooton's closed its doors in 1995. At the time of closure, Tooton's had stores all over the city and the province.

Some of the Brazil Street families in my day were the Whites, Murphys, Chipmans, Hayeses, Hearns, Bishops, Barrons, Shorts, Zimmermans, Englishes, Bucks, and Byrnes. They were Protestants, Roman Catholics, and Jews. We Catholics frowned on the other religions—their way was not the "true way." Such were the times.

Number 40, the house where I lived for twenty-one years (until I married and moved out), was at the bottom of the street. It was sold to us by a family named Lush. It needed a lot of work, but it was comfortable. (Mom made it a home with her magic, as all mothers seem to do.) The house was three storeys high and listed to the left, as though it were slowly sinking into the ground sideways; obviously, it had been built on an uneven foundation. It was joined to number 38, the Whites' house. On the other side was a small laneway that led to our twenty-by-forty-foot garden, where we played hockey all winter, starting as soon as it was cold enough for water to freeze.

As you entered the front door you were met by the stairs leading to the upstairs rooms. To the right of the stairs was a twelve-foot hallway that led to a small living room and the kitchen. To the right of the kitchen was a hatch which you went through to get to the coal cellar. The bathroom, my parents' bedroom, and Edward's bedroom were on the second floor. Calvin, Hubert, Angus, and I slept in the third-storey attic. Being the youngest, Hubert and Angus shared a bed; the rest of us had our own beds. My bedroom in the farthest part of the attic adjoined the bedrooms of my brothers.

The house was heated by coal, and then by oil. I remember a horse-drawn coal wagon coming to the house and dropping a half-ton of coal down the chute into our cellar. We used to take buckets of the coal upstairs for the stove, which had to be checked several times during the night to make sure the fire hadn't gone out. The house was always freezing during the winter; often we went to sleep with severe, biting cold air in the house. Many nights, despite a cocoon of sheets and at least four large blankets, my teeth chattered and the rest of me shook, up there in bed on the third floor. A half-inch of frost would accumulate on the windows when the temperature dipped below freezing, and sometimes it dipped well below that. During the summer months, the heat in the house was unbearable. In those days we had fantastic summers, with temperatures between ninety and a hundred degrees Fahrenheit for days on end.

During the latter part of the 1960s oil took the place of coal, and most houses had an oil tank out back. My brothers and I took turns going to the tank and filling up a one-gallon container with oil. It didn't matter what the weather was like or what time of day it was, you had to take your turn getting oil for the stove.

When it snowed, we had plenty of it, sometimes piled up to the second-storey window of our three-storey house. After breakfast on a day after a big snowfall, we had to go out through the window in Dad's room and shovel downward until we reached the front door, and then we would shovel our way to the sidewalk. This usually took several hours. I used to think I would be shovelling forever, I was so small, but with my father and my brothers pitching in, the snow finally got cleared away. We had tons of snow all winter long, and the winters seemed endless. Everyone complains these days when we have a storm, but our winters today are nothing compared to what we had in those days.

All the houses on our street were attached. If there was ever a serious fire, the whole block would have gone up in smoke very quickly. Luckily, we never did have any major fires when I lived there, although I spent many nights in my third-storey bedroom thinking about how I would escape. It was a long drop to the ground, about thirty feet.

I always wondered how Dad and Mom made ends meet. I thought my parents were magicians, feeding and clothing five boys on one small salary. And my mother wasn't able to do much work because of her heart. Most of the men in that area had labour jobs and worked very hard for the money they did earn. Getting by was a common struggle; every penny went toward the support of the household.

With five boys in the house and not much money to live on, food was never wasted. And you either ate what was offered or went hungry. You ate what was put in front of you, and you didn't complain. There were two choices: eat or go hungry. Many nights I came home late to no supper because I was out gallivanting somewhere, and my brothers had eaten it all.

The same food was served on the same nights every week. Liver, sausages, black puddings. Fish was a staple—we ate it several times a week because it was cheap. We lived on fish and molasses and homemade bread. Sunday was the best food day because we usually had turkey, with dressing; you never missed Sunday dinner or Sunday night's cold plate. To this day I never hold back when buying groceries. I can still remember not having enough to eat as a teenager, and I swore that when I had money of my own I would eat whatever I wanted.

Our bread was always made by Mom; Dad used to knead it for her if he was home, because of her bad heart. Bread was what we usually had for breakfast. Bread and tea. We would toast it over the open flame from the oven. It was what we had for our school lunches, too. Bread with butter, or sometimes with peanut butter.

****

My parents were devout Roman Catholics. "Non-practicing" was unheard of, among Catholics at least. I had a Protestant friend who lived across the street from us, and he was treated as an outsider. My father told us that it was probably okay to "knock around" with him, but that if he discussed religion with us we were to ignore what he said. His religion wasn't the true religion, my father told us, and my friend and his family were not likely to go to heaven. My father wasn't cruel; he was just a product of his time, class, and religion. My parents and their parents had the Roman Catholic religion beaten into them, and it was beaten into us. Quite literally. We had no choice but to believe: unbelief was the way to damnation, and a hot, dark spot in hell!

There was always a deep sense of religion in the Roman Catholic family home in those days. You wouldn't dare skip church on Sunday. If your parents found out you hadn't gone, you paid dearly for it. We were always given money for the collection plate, but the Church never made it rich off Dickie or me. We spent it on candy at Power's store on the way to Mass, or coming back from it.

You had to remember what was preached from the Gospel every Sunday, because one of your parents might question you about it. That didn't happen every week, but if it did, and you didn't know what the sermon had been about, your parents would know you hadn't gone to church that morning. (My mother's heart condition prevented her from making the walk to the church, which was on Patrick Street; my father went to early-morning Mass.) So, Dickie and I took turns going to church. Whoever went would leave right after the sermon and tell the other about it, in case our parents asked questions.

In May, we knelt in one of the rooms of the house every night and said the Rosary, like other Catholic families. This was in honour of the Blessed Virgin; Catholics dedicate the month of May to her devotion. If we laughed or fooled around, we got a cuff from Dad or Mom, whoever was the closest. My brothers and I couldn't wait for it to end each night. We hated it. After all, we were only kids and religion didn't hold the same meaning for us that it did for the adults.

****

Dickie and I became street smart at a very early age. We figured out that there was always some cash to be had—somewhere and everywhere! Most of us poor kids found ways to get money for some of the things that we wanted.

I went to school many times without enough money in my pocket for a snack. One day Dickie and I decided that the only way to stop being poor was to beg, borrow, or steal our share of the things that the well-off kids in school had. But begging, borrowing, and stealing were out if we could do an honest day's work for money.

Dickie and I always had one scam or another going for us, although we put on the poor face to our friends so they would think we were penniless. But money was to be made; you just had to figure out how, and make it work for you. You had to make choices. Choices gave you an opportunity to change things.

In the back of our house, at the end of White's garden, we built a small clubhouse, which we added to every year. The clubhouse was between four and five feet in height, fifteen feet in length, and about six feet wide. It had two sections divided by a piece of cloth. The foundation was built out of rough old wood, scraps from the lumberyard on Gower Street. The sides were made of heavy cardboard from the thick breadboxes that came from Walsh's Bakery. The floor was also made out of these boxes. It was here that we held council on everything that happened to us, and many of our money-making schemes were born. During the summer months, we practically lived in this old dilapidated lean-to, and many nights our parents let us sleep there. With a watchful eye on us, for sure. Each year we would rebuild it after the winter, and add to it as the club's membership grew, but basically it was frequented mostly by Dickie and me. It became our home away from home.

It was in our backyard clubhouse that Dickie and I came up with "Orphan Lake." It was an idea, a fantasy, that took us away from the poverty of our lives. We considered ourselves as poor as the orphans of Mount Cashel (we didn't realize that those boys were living and eating better than we were, but we also didn't know about the abuse). And so we envisioned ourselves living beside a peaceful lake, where everything was plentiful and we had no worries. Orphan Lake was something to look forward to in the future as we struggled in the present. Orphan Lake was where we would end up some day, a heaven where we had money and lived the way the rich kids did. No poverty, no hunger, no handouts. And we would never have to work again. Boy, were we ever naive!

We used to say that the children at our school who had everything they needed and more (things we could only dream of having) had already found their Orphan Lake, and that some day we would find ours. Dickie and I had to go without many of the pleasures of life because our families could not afford them. Even when we were older, we used to refer to Orphan Lake whenever we saw a wealthy person, or someone who seemed to have everything they wanted. We would look at each other and smile and say, "They found their Orphan Lake."

When Dickie died, I thought about Orphan Lake at his wake. About how he had likely found it at last.

****

Halfway down Brazil Street, where Monroe Street intersects, was Vera Buck's convenience store. Vera was a widow who lived by herself. She liked her drink and was absent-minded, but she was generous. Not only to her regulars, but to everyone who entered her store. About twenty of us boys protected her. She was safe from strangers, drunk or sober, as long as we were around. We spent a lot of time at Vera's store, always getting into a good game of cards—120s (also called growl). She always let us run up tabs, without keeping track of half of what we bought. But we always made sure that everything we owed was paid back, with a little extra for the loan.

There were a lot of characters around that part of St. John's in those days. Two of the most famous were the Mullins sisters, Kathleen and Patsy. The Mullins sisters were between ten and fifteen years older than I was. As far as I can remember, Patsy lived on Bully Street and Kathleen lived with a Mrs. Shirley Ready on Prince Street. Mom and Dad always warned us to stay away from them when they were drinking.

Patsy was a very large lady. She weighed about 200 pounds, and she was very strong. She was chubby, not fat, and had a rough look about her. Her hair was dark and she had fair skin. She was always in trouble with the RNC, for vagrancy and drinking in public. She was a menacing enough figure sober, but when she was drinking she was as tough as they came. Her sister Kathleen was taller and not quite as heavy, but she was solid. She could beat any man who was crazy enough to fight her. Many a police officer and sailor came out on the losing side when they tried to out-duel or out-drink either of the Mullins sisters.

Drinking did terrible things to Patsy and Kathleen. Ask any police officer of that era, and he would tell you he would rather have been called out alone to a fight involving six men rather than face either of the Mullins sisters, especially Kathleen. In those days if you were a police officer, you had absolute authority (like anyone else in authority back then). You used it to look after the city, and maintain law and order. But sometimes vigilante justice was dished out in the streets by those authorities. Young people, like my friends and me, were afraid of police officers, and of the Black Maria, the police van that patrolled the city streets day and night. If you were put in the Maria, you were sure to get a few smacks in the gob, or generally roughed up.

Patsy and Kathleen often ended up in the Black Maria when they were drunk or in a fight, but they weren't the ones who received rough handling. It was the police officers who had bruises and cuts the next day from an encounter with one or both of them. Sometimes it took three or four of them to get one of the sisters into the van. Kathleen was always the harder of the two to calm down.

A man I knew foolishly tried to take a bottle from Kathleen one night when she was sitting, apparently fast asleep, with her back to the wall of Leo Hogan's store on the corner of Casey and Brazil. He was soon knocked on his rear end when he went to take the bottle from inside her coat. He was also given a few good belts. He got them from Kathleen, as a reminder not to go near her or her liquor again while she was napping. She had no more trouble with him. I remember when Patsy was arrested for breaking into the liquor store on Water Street—she smashed the main window out late one night. They found her passed out drunk on the floor.

When they weren't drinking, the Mullins sisters were the easiest women in the world to get along with. One day I passed Kathleen sitting on a bench on Water Street, and she stopped me and asked if I had any money. She was hungry. I asked her what she wanted to eat and she said, "A hamburger." I went into Woolworths, where I was working at the time, and got her a large burger and fries and a soft drink. She devoured the meal, spilling half of it all over herself. She said I was a nice boy for getting her a treat, and if anyone ever hit me or otherwise hurt me to let her know, and she would make sure it would never happen again. She described what she would do to them, and it wasn't pleasant.

After that, Kathleen never said anything mean to me or my brothers when she was drunk. We always gave a helping hand to her and Patsy when we could. She called us "the nice Hunt boys." My brothers and my father and mother pitied her. My parents told us to be careful of the Mullins sisters when they were drinking, but to treat them respectfully. They were human beings like us, who had taken the wrong path in life but were still God's children.

I was told that both sisters eventually died in the Waterford Hospital, Patsy from cancer and Kathleen from Alzheimer's. I also heard that Kathleen's two sons went to the mainland and found good jobs there. Patsy had no children.

Patsy and Kathleen had two brothers, who were much tamer than their sisters. I can't remember much about Harry, except that he was an electrician. The other brother, Tommy, was a bit simple; he seemed like a little boy trapped in a man's body. I remember him coming to Woolworths when I worked there, to wash employees' cars. We would give him some money, or buy him something to eat, or give him candy from the candy counter. He always said the same thing when he left us: "I'm going to see Father Pat now, for supper." One of the parish priests must have looked out for him.

****

Phones were not in common use in St. John's until the 1950s. In the beginning, our family shared a phone line with other people—a party line. Our first phone number was 4959-F. On a party line, you could hear other people's conversations and they could hear yours, so you had to be careful; people listening in would gossip about what was being said. One of the main topics of conversation was the poor Mullins sisters, of course, and what they had done the night before.

We kids used to have a ball on the party line. (We lived in houses where the walls were so thin that everybody could listen to everybody else's conversations anyway. Gossip was a staple of life; it helped stave off the boredom of poverty.) Dickie and I used to get on the line and make up things about Patsy and Kathleen—to their benefit—because we knew it would be added to the gossip. We said we heard that the Mullins sisters were really from a rich family, and that was how they got the money for drinking. Or that Mr. and Mrs. So-and-So, relatives of theirs, owned a large general store in Clarenville, and they gave money to Patsy and Kathleen. No one on the line had any way of knowing if what was said was truth or fiction. Our rumours spread like wildfire, and people started to leave the Mullins sisters alone.

Another character of the day was a man called Silly Willy. The poor guy roamed the streets of St. John's in an old overcoat for many years. He was a harmless old man, but we were afraid of him because he would growl at us when we walked by him. I never did hear of him hurting anyone, though.

One man would jump and curse at you and call you awful names when you walked or drove by him and shouted "Hey!" Which was why his nickname was "Hey." Rumour had it that he had been shell-shocked in World War II. If he had something in his hands when you shouted at him, he would throw it at you. We heard poor Hey ended up in the Waterford Hospital, which was likely where he ended his days.

Another character who used to roam the streets was a guy named Mickey Doyle. He frequented the Mundy Pond area and the downtown for years. A friend of mine, Judy Cranford, and her friend, Carol Ann Escott, found him frozen to death in Glasgow's (an open field by Mundy Pond) one winter.

Other notable characters of the day were Pinky Skanes, Bucky King (now immortalized on a mural on Duckworth Street), and Billy Cox. These people were a constant source of gossip. We heard many tales about such-and-such a person doing this or that. Hardly any of it was true. It was just a way of relieving boredom.

mom and dad

My mother, Carmel Mary Hayes, was born in 1918 in Port Royal, Long Island, Placentia Bay, a community that became part of the post-Confederation Resettlement Program. Like most women in those days, she was a stay-at-home mother, who had her hands full caring for five boys while her husband was away, which was most of the time.

Mom was a small woman, about five-two, and a tiny one. She had blackish-grey hair and a pretty face, oval with high cheekbones; I remember her as looking something like Queen Elizabeth. She was always smiling. I can't remember the colour of her eyes, but I do remember that they were soft, like her voice. She spoke almost in a whisper; we often had to ask her to speak up. My mother wore glasses for as long as I can remember, and dresses like most women of her era.

She had a heart condition that was a result of rheumatic fever, and this condition, besides keeping her thin, gave her face an eerie white look. Her movements were awkward and slow, and she was always tired. She couldn't walk for a long time without resting. As she got older and her condition worsened, she started to lose her looks; her face became drawn and haggard. It took her about half an hour to walk upstairs to her room. We kids had to help her navigate the steep climb, one step at a time. At the time of her death, she hadn't been to our bedrooms on the third floor for years.

Before he went away to work, Dad would warn us to take care of her while he was gone. He was very protective of Mom and always watched over her. Heaven would have had to protect anyone who said anything mean to her, because Dad was very strict and tough when it came to my mother.

Mom had an air about her that everyone in the neighbourhood loved. Kind and generous to a fault, she was a good, God-fearing woman, well-liked by everyone who met her. She treated everyone equally and with the greatest of respect, and people always had a kind word for her. Everyone came to Mom with their problems, knowing they would get a kind word and a friendly smile. I never heard her utter a curse word once, even when she was angry, which was rare. That must have been a very hard thing to do, not to swear; ordinary life was trying enough in those times, and she had five boys to look after, often by herself, and a severe heart condition. She never seemed to get mad at anything or anyone, though. She was a quiet, patient woman.

When she did become ticked off at us, she used an expression I've never heard anyone else use. On the rare occasions when she hit the boiling point, she would call us "flenting flamers." Other than that, her favourite curse word was "sugar."

People in the neighbourhood could ask Mom for

anything, and she would do whatever was in her power to accommodate them. She never said no to anyone. My mother was one in a million.

On the night of July 27, 1967, I was visiting a friend on Pleasant Street when Valentine "Val" Grouchy told me that my dad wanted me to come home. My mother was in the hospital, but I didn't think of that as I ran to the house, a few blocks away. I stood outside our house for a moment, looking in.

The night was as silent as a church during the serving of Communion. I will never forget the sight of Dad sitting at the kitchen table with his head down, crying. I knew then what had happened. My mother had been in Toronto General Hospital for nearly a year, where she underwent open-heart surgery (probably for a valve replacement), and she had been admitted to St. Clare's Hospital on her return. She had come back from Toronto for about two months at one point, but complications forced her to go back. When she was finally sent back to us, we thought that the worst was over. She could walk without any difficulty, and she seemed to be on the mend.

I stood outside the house for what seemed like an eternity, my small world crashing down upon me. I could actually feel the pain that Dad was in. When I went in my father looked at me and said two words, the same two words he had spoken to my older brother Edward just a few minutes earlier. "She's gone." His eyes said everything else. He was staring at a picture of her in his hands. And then he laid the picture down and put his hands up to his face, crying openly.

The day of my mother's death was the roughest day

of her sons' young lives, and a day that I have lived with for many years. It was the day I found out that life is unpredictable and dangerous. When she died, I was eighteen, and my brothers' ages ranged from ten to twenty.

My father was never the same after my mother's death. He seemed to be in a mild state of shock until his death in 1990. When she died, a large part of him died with her; a void was created that he would never be able to fill. He had lost his soulmate.

Come Home Year was 1966, the year before she died. My mother had wanted her brothers and sisters to come back to Newfoundland for a visit that year, but Dad told her it was better if they waited until 1967—she might feel well enough by then to entertain them all. But come home they did anyway, and enjoyed a wonderful last time with my mother.

After Mom died, Dad hired a lady named Mrs. Florence Hickey to look after the household. She was a wonderful, gentle woman who remained with us for several years. She could never take Mom's place, but she was magic in the kitchen for baking, and she took good care of us all. We enjoyed every moment she was with us, and we hated to see her leave at night. She had a great personality, and was a very kind and good-natured. It couldn't have been easy dealing with six men and their many faults.

****

My father, Edward Hunt, hailed from Harbour Breton on the south coast of Newfoundland; he was born in

1912. He moved to St. John's after he was transferred from the coastal boats to a porter's job on the trains sometime after World War II ended, probably in 1947. He met my mother when the coastal boat he was on went into port in Placentia Bay. It was the start of a romance that would last a lifetime.

Dad was a short man, only about five feet, six inches tall, but he was broad-shouldered and strong as a bull and built like a brick wall; he could have been a wrestler. He wore glasses and didn't have much hair, but his piercing green eyes and rough features were very intimidating. One look at Dad, and most guys walked the other way. His hands were huge. I remember thinking I would never try to engage him in a fight; those who did usually ended up on their backs. Short and strong and quick, that was my Dad. He was very protective of his wife and his sons.

Despite his physical attributes, Dad was a gentle, kind-hearted man who worked very hard. As far as I know, my father never went beyond grade five, but that wasn't uncommon at the time. Most young men of his generation and class had to go to work at a young age; education was a luxury back then. Regardless, Dad was a smart man who always knew what was going on in the world.

During World War II, while he was in the Canadian Merchant Navy, he was on a ship when it was torpedoed near Dover, England. He spent several days on a piece of wreckage before being rescued, and then several weeks in an English hospital. Thirty-three men out of the ninety-two on board the ship survived the torpedo attack. My father came back home with severe migraine headaches, from which he suffered nearly every day of his life.

Only once did he speak of what happened to him. It was Christmas Day, and he was having a few drinks with me and some of my friends. We asked him to tell us about the war. Dickie egged him on, and Dad finally said, "Okay, Dickie, you and your friends have been asking me about the war for years, so here it is."

He had left St. John's on a ship bound for Dover. The second day out, they were struck by two torpedoes. When he was about halfway through his story and well into his third or fourth drink of rum—and Dad didn't drink very much—he started to cry. He had suffered a very traumatic event, made even more traumatic by the loss of friends and shipmates.

We started to wish that we hadn't bought up the subject of the sinking, because it obviously pained him terribly to talk about it. We could see the sorrow etched in his face and realized he must have been suffering inwardly for many years. That Christmas Day it all flowed. We were glad when he finished his story, and we never asked for it again.

No one ever pushed Dad around or told him what to do. He always held his own against those who tried to take advantage of Ned Hunt. He and Mom were devoutly religious, and they would never intentionally harm anyone. But if you hurt Ned Hunt's family, then you had better watch out—because you had just hurt him! He was called "sir" when he needed to be, and his respect for other people earned him good friendships. Being poor never bothered him in the least. He knew who he was and where he had come from, and he never forgot.

Dad rarely hit us or disciplined us severely. I can remember very few occasions on which he got really angry at something that I did. When I was about six years old, I broke a window, smashing it with my hand and screaming for Mom. She had locked the downstairs door before going upstairs to visit our McKay Street neighbour. I kept banging away at the window and screaming, and I finally broke it. When Dad arrived home he was mad as hell. He shouted at me for being so stupid. Replacing that window was something they could not easily afford.

Once he smacked me on the rear end in the course of trying to push me into my bedroom; I was being sent to bed early as punishment for something or other. When he smacked me, I fell and hooked my leg into the springs of a daybed, and ended up hitting my head on a small coal bucket. My eye started to swell out like a balloon. My father felt terrible. He ended up rocking me in his arms until I went to sleep. I had a shiner for about a week, but I was proud of it. It was something to show off to my friends in school, although I didn't tell them what really happened. I bragged that I had been in a fight, and had beaten the other guy up!

Another time, when I was about eight or nine, the family was sitting at the table, about to have supper. In those days you didn't eat a meal without saying a prayer beforehand, a blessing for the food that Dad had worked so hard to provide for us. My mother had to stop saying the blessing to reprimand me for laughing and joking. In the heat of the moment, I said something saucy back to her. Dad backhanded me across the face for speaking to Mom that way, and all I saw were stars for about ten minutes, lying there on the kitchen floor.

Other than on those two occasions, I don't remember him ever hitting me or my brothers. Perhaps a little smack on the backside when it was deserved, but that was about it. Other boys and girls our age were often beaten by their parents, and it was usually liquor-related. We were just lucky that we had Mom and Dad for parents.

On Sunday nights, Dad's friends Bert and Mary Hayes, Basil and Margaret Meaney, and Ches and Dorothy Chipman would come to the house for a game of growl. The further they got into the game and the liquor, the louder they got. The shouts of laughter rolled up from downstairs into our bedrooms.

Dad was an excellent accordion player. After the card game, he would take out the accordion and either Basil or Ches would play the mouth organ. We went to sleep listening to the music, or the rapping of knuckles on the card table (signifying that a thirty-for-sixty score had been made). We would fall off into dreamland listening to those sounds, and everything in our little world was all right.

In the summer of 1958, Dad took us on a trip to his hometown of Harbour Breton. Before 1965, going any distance was a difficult thing to do because the main highway was only a dirt road. Passage on it was cumbersome and rough, and it took a very long time to get anywhere.

Since Dad didn't drive, we had to hire an out-of-town taxi to go to Argentia. On the Placentia highway, the taxi was stopped by the RCMP and we were told that a forest fire was raging out of control ahead. We were to pull in and wait until the all-clear sign was given. Though the fire wasn't near the highway, high winds were threatening to move it closer. We ended up waiting for at least two hours on the side of the road. I remember seeing the fire lighting up the forest in the distance as darkness started to settle, after we got back on the road.

When we arrived in Argentia, we had to wait another hour or so for the ferry to leave—the *Bar Haven*, which would take us to Harbour Breton. It was waiting for others who were delayed because of the forest fire. Finally we set out to sea, which was starting to become a little rough. We stood with the rest of the passengers at the rail, watching the blaze of the forest fire.

When we were halfway to our destination, we ran into a storm that tossed the *Bar Haven* about as if it were a paper ship. The waves came in over the deck, and I could hear Dad telling Mom not to worry: he had seen worse weather than this when he was working on the CN coastal boats, he said. I don't think that relieved Mom's mind at all. I'll never forget the look of concern on her face, concern for her children's safety as the storm raged and the ship tossed on the open sea.

The boat rocked back and forth for what seemed like an eternity. I thought that the sinking of the ship was inevitable. Someone walking by the cabin we were in stopped to talk to Dad, and he told Mom to say a prayer that the weather would calm down and that we would get safely across. My brothers and I became very seasick; the last thing I remember that night was lying down in the cabin by my mother's feet with a blanket over me.

The next thing I remember was waking up to a calm sea, and Mom and Dad saying that the storm was over and that we were safe. For a boy of my age, it was like a fantasy from a comic book. My brothers and I spoke of it for years afterwards to anyone who would listen.

****

When my brothers and I were in our fifties, we talked of going to Port Royal, to step on the land where Mom grew up, and to revisit an area we had visited many times as young children.

In 2003 we did just that, although only Calvin, Hubert, and I were able to make the journey. It was a beautiful excursion, and a better time we could not have asked for than the three days we spent there. The weather was beautiful—eighty to ninety degrees for those three precious days. It was as if Mom knew that we were coming to visit her, and she had set the stage for us with bright skies and pleasant weather.

In order to get to Port Royal, we had to go by boat down Placentia Bay for about two and a half hours, passing Merasheen Island and many of the smaller resettled islands along the way. We left from Come By Chance with our first cousin Kate Barry and her husband, Lou Baker, in the thirty-foot boat Lou and another person had built. The trip down Placentia Bay was worth the forty-odd-year wait, the sea spray skipping in over the deck and all of us breathing in the fresh, salt air. It was as if we were on another planet. We listened to the boat humming along in the water, in complete harmony with the sound of the waves striking it.

After landing at Port Royal, the first thing we did was walk to the place where Mom had lived, about a mile or so from where we docked. The house was long gone, but Kate showed us where it had been. It was an amazing feeling, standing where she and her brothers and sisters had once lived and played. The house was situated on a hillside overlooking the bay. On what would have been the back of the house is a cliff, about 200 feet above the water. My brothers and I talked about how my mother and her siblings must have been warned many times by our grandparents not to play on its dangerous ledges.

I had brought some soil from Mom's and Dad's graves (both, of course, were buried in the same plot in St. John's), and I buried it where Mom's house had once stood. It was a sort of coming-home gesture. There are many graveyards on the island, and some of the stones date back to the 1700s. Relatives from the past who never left the island.

the corner boy area

The area surrounding New Gower Street was our particular territory growing up. The bottom of Brazil Square (where the Delta Hotel now stands) was our main playground. Brazil Square, which no longer exists, was at the lower end of Brazil Street; it extended down into New Gower Street. Casey Street branches off Brazil, intersecting John Street, Haggerty Street, and Springdale Street to the west, and Central Street and McFarlane (Flower Hill) to the east. These streets were our domain for more than two decades.

Sometimes we would wander over to other streets, such as Barter's Hill (where we hung out in Martin's Meadow, a lumberyard) or one of the many other streets that bordered our area—Central, Livingstone, Lime, Monroe, and Cabot. But mainly we stayed in our own little area and never encroached on other guys' turfs. To do so could lead to a fight.

In those days Brazil Square was sort of like a city within a city. Except for a few businesses, it was made up of mostly boarding houses that charged minimal rates for a night's stay. Its nickname was "baymen's paradise." A lot of people who came to St. John's from rural Newfoundland—on business, to visit relatives, to attend Memorial University, or for medical reasons—stayed in boarding houses on Brazil Square. (The rivalry between "townies" and "baymen" was fierce in those days. People said baymen came into town to take jobs away from us. That didn't stop us from dating the out-of-town girls, however.) Some of the boarding houses of that era were Eddy's, Dean's, Batt's, Tucker's, and the Brownsdale Hotel. We always had a cousin or someone from outside St. John's staying with us while they were in town working or going to university. (MUN was situated on Parade Street until 1961.) My cousins Isabel Dicks from Rushoon and Cyril and Kevin Barry from Port Royal stayed with us every summer. Isabel and Marion Augot, from Dad's home of Harbour Breton, stayed with us when they went to MUN.

Kenney's Fruit Store was opposite the Brownsdale Hotel, at the bottom of the Square. At the top of the Square was White's Fish and Chips, and Higgins' store. Local businesses made a good living from people who came into the city. Glasco's Meat Market on Brazil Square was in competition with Casey's Meat Market around the corner on New Gower Street. Bob Glasco was a good, kind-hearted man for whom I worked part-time while I went to school. Many times I heard him tell customers who were short of money to pay him some other time. I'm sure that in the year and a half I worked for him he was owed a fortune, but I never heard him ask anyone for money.

Jack Kidney's shoe repair was next door to

Glasco's. Jack was a distinguished man, with long grey hair, always smoking a pipe. He was self-educated, well-informed, articulate, and always open to discussion about any news of the day. He could hold his own in conversation with anybody in the neighbourhood on any topic, especially when it came to politics. My father would always stop in and talk to Jack when he went to Brazil Square on business. Jack did wonderful shoe repairs, and could make a pair of John Whites last a family of five forever.

The Salvation Army was very much a part of the scene. Its members would gather around the telephones poles on Brazil Square and sing hymns. People used to drop money for the poor into a small collection plate. The Army was revered by people in those days because it was always there to help anyone in need, regardless of their religious beliefs. Its members made home visits and sacrificed what little they had to help others. They would literally give you the shirts off their backs.

We used to congregate on Haggerty Street. We spent many nights sliding down its steep hill without any worry of cars getting in our way; in those days, not too many people could afford to drive one, especially in that neighbourhood. We were one level above being truly poor.

But the corner was our main hangout. We would meet there at least once or twice during the week, even on school nights, and every weekend. The boys and girls from the area got together to talk—often into the wee hours of the night—about music, friends, jobs, school, sports, and anything else that was fit for conversation. Girls talked about boys, boys talked about girls, both talked about breakups and reunions. The corner was where everyone went to swap stories about how their lives were going, what problems they were having, and how things were changing and were going to continue to change. We headed to the corner whenever we wanted to hold a powwow about life. I met my friends there from age eight to twenty-seven. I think those meetings affected everyone's life in some way. They certainly influenced mine. Friendship meant a lot in those days. Little did we know that lifelong relationships and even marriages would result from these tribal get-togethers.

Dickie and I were exclusive members of the corner, and my brothers were corner regulars. Other members included Tommy Dodd; Paul Fleming; David White and Harold White Jr. (Dickie's younger brothers); Willie Rodden; Ronnie Glasco; Dave and George Bishop; Bob Janes; Dougie, Val, and Bobby Grouchy; Dave Williams; Tommy Brewer; Dave and Terry Murphy; Jim Peddle; Dave Rumsey; Johnny Breen; Paddy Evans; George Smith; Edward and Fred Sweeney; Mike Lynch; Frank and Fred "Butch" Reddy; Harry and Gordie Husk; Ed and Jimmy King; Paul, Jack, Walter, and Frank Barrington from Quidi Vidi; Ron Lacey; Bo Lee; Bruce Murrin; Johnny Raymond; Rick, Fred, and Johnny Barela; Spider Young; Jerry Coady; Paul Crane; Walter Butt; Tony and Chris Jesso; Charlie and Paul O'Dea; Paddy Adams; Bobby Holwell; Herbie and Macky White; Ray Meadus; Paddy Harding; and Bobby Gulliver.

Some of the female "corner girls" were Cynthia

Williams, Rose and Sharon O'Leary, Fran Winsor, Marie Taylor, Jean White, Sharon and Donna Cooney, Louise and Laura White (Dickie's sisters), Carol Glasco, Gwen Williams, Gail Hearn, Rose Moriarty, Megan Williams, and Shirley and Barbara Sweeney.

Some were corner members for only a short time, and there were others, too, whose names I have forgotten. Some corner boys and girls are dead now: Jim Peddle, Dave Hillier, Jerry Coady, Cynthia Williams, Marie Taylor, and Sharon Cooney. (Sharon Cooney later became my sister-in-law, when she married my younger brother Hubert.)

I will never forget the night Cynthia Williams died. It was a summer evening in July, 1966. We were all standing on the corner talking about school and other things when we heard that Cynthia had been rushed to St. Clare's Mercy Hospital with a severe pain in one side of her body. She was examined and released. A few hours later she was rushed back to the hospital, where she died from a ruptured appendix. The whole corner was in shock. It was the first time that a member of our group of friends had died. It took us years to get over it; Cynthia was spoken of many times in the course of our long talks on the corner.

John Street was another area, where we sometimes hung around with friends. Some families that lived on John Street were the Sweeneys, Williamses, O'Deas, Jackmans, Jessos, Husks, O'Learys, and Brewers. Dickie and I used to go to a store on John Street that was owned by Patrick and Maggie Flynn. Flynn's Grocery was on the eastern side of John, sandwiched in between the Sweeneys' house and the Williamses'.

Dickie and I used to drive poor old Paddy and Maggie Flynn absolutely crazy. We used to go to Paddy's store to buy things we needed, and we also "borrowed" a few things from him when he wasn't looking. I'm sure he used to cringe when he saw Dickie and me heading toward his beloved store, especially when we started to work and make money, and had a charge account there.

Paddy, timid and very easily excited, would stand behind the counter while Maggie shouted from the top of the stairs: "What do those boys from up the road want?" or "Don't be long now, Paddy, I want you to get something for me!" It was always the same scenario when we went to see him. I'm sure he and Maggie had it planned beforehand. They both had good hearts, though.

When Dickie and I were about nine or ten years old, we discovered a new and dangerous hobby: clinging to the backs of oil trucks as they went up Casey Street in the winter. The trucks had big steel bumpers, complete with chain links, which we used to hold on to as the trucks slowly made their way up the street. One night as Dickie, Willie Rodden, and I were gliding up the street on the back of a truck, Dickie's foot hooked into a rut in the street and he lost his balance and his hold on the truck. He slipped face down onto the pavement, hurting his shoulder pretty badly and scratching up his face and hands. We took him the few blocks to St. Clare's, where a nurse examined him and asked us what had happened. Dickie told her he was jumped by three guys and that *they* had taken a beating. On the way home, he added some details to this story—that he had been alone and some guys from the other side of town had fought him for survival. This, or something like it, was what he told his parents. (When Dickie told a lie, he was so convincing that it actually sounded like the truth. Not that he was a hard-core liar—we all had to tell small lies sometimes, to save our skins.)

The next day we went to Paddy Flynn's store. Paddy and Maggie, having heard the story about poor Dickie being jumped and beaten up, gave both of us a free lunch complete with Dutch Creams and Double Colas. (Of course, I told them I was involved in the fighting so that I could get a lunch too.) Good old Paddy and Maggie, what lovely people! When we were old enough to drink, Dickie and I used to talk about the old days at Flynn's store over a few cold ones. Poor Paddy was ruled by Maggie, but he always found a way to treat us well. He felt sorry for us when we were kids because we didn't have much money, and he always gave us a little extra when we bought candy or pastries.

When we started working he allowed us to extend our credit line beyond what Maggie deemed acceptable. He would hide the notes with the extra charges on them underneath the counter.

Dickie and I were very fond of Graham Sandwiches, little wafer bars covered with chocolate. If Paddy was out of them, we would pester him to order more, and he would put us out of the store. When I went to work for Coca-Cola and Dickie started working for city council, we always left a few extra dollars on the counter when we went to Paddy's to buy something. Paddy knew we were paying him back for the things we had "borrowed" from him over the years.

The last I heard of Paddy Flynn was that when Maggie died in the early 1970s, he moved away to some place in the United States where a son or daughter lived.

Another thing some of my friends and I "borrowed" were bottles, from the boarding houses on Brazil Square. A group of us would check the back gardens of these houses, hoping that there were pop, beer, or liquor bottles there, which we would grab and turn in at the stores for a few pennies. We spent many a night jumping over fences and claiming our prizes.

One of our favourite places to raid was Eddy's. At least once a week, Old Man Eddy (I think his first name was Clar) would put out his pop or rum bottles and keep an eye out for us, knowing we would be after them. Looking back at it now, it seems to me it was a little game between him and us. Often, we were caught as soon as we made it over the fence. If he did catch us, he would just give us a swift kick in the rear end and send us on our way. No phoning the police—in those days, it was frontier justice!

One Monday night—Monday night was a good night for a raid; many bottles were put out behind the houses after the weekend—we decided that Willie Rodden would be the lookout while we took Old Man Eddy's bottles. My brother Hubert, Willie, Bob Janes, Paul Barrington, and I were the culprits that night. Willie peeked through a knot in the fence door while we rummaged through piles of refuse for bottles. Bang! Mr. Eddy, who was waiting for us behind the door of his house, kicked it open. Willie fell to the ground, and Mr. Eddy came at us like a charging bull. Poor Willie was lying on the ground with his hands up to his face, which was all scratched and bloody. We realized then that we had hit Mr. Eddy on a bad night. He was a big man. We scattered like flies.

Willie managed to climb the fence while one of the others and I pushed Mr. Eddy to the ground. Then it was a mad dash up and over his ten-foot fence.

Learn a lesson? Hell, no. We stayed away from Eddy's for a week or two, and then we decided to raid it again. When we got there, we found that he had cut part of a tree away for us so that we could get into the garden without climbing his fence. When we thought about it years later, we realized that he was more concerned about his new fence than the bottles. There were always bottles there after that. I guess he thought it was better to join us than to fight us. But as I said, it must have been a game with him, because he knew who we were and he could have told our parents what was going on—that would have quickly put an end to our sport.

We sometimes unloaded our bottles at Mr. Noftall's on Barron Street (off Casey) for what little money we could get. Mr. Noftall was an old man who lived in a dilapidated house; he collected junk and soft drink and beer bottles to sell. Bob "Bottles" Janes got his nickname from stealing bottles back from Noftall after he had sold them to him, and reselling them to Noftall the next day or a few days later. Bottles Janes was a cool customer, all right!

Our playground was spread out in those days, but the New Gower Street area was a favourite of Dickie's and mine when we were looking for adventure. It was always a source of odd jobs, and without those jobs we wouldn't have had a cent.

The lower part of New Gower next to Brazil Square became my haven. Hogan's Drugstore, George Street United Church, Casey's Meat Market, and other small businesses were on the lower side. Opposite these were Chaulker's, a popular fish-and-chip take-out, and Harris's barbershop; Parson's store was on the bottom corner of Pleasant Street, and Kenney's fruit store and the Belmont Club were on the opposite corner. Farther west, down the side of Springdale Street, were Horwood's lumberyard, J. B. Hand's retail outlet, Power's store, and Marty's fish-and-chip shop. Harding's Trucking was at the bottom of Springdale Street.

Farther east on New Gower Street, past the Belmont Club, was Lars' fruit store, now Breen's; they're still selling his famous custard cones, which cost ten cents fifty years ago. Buckingham's hardware store stood on the corner of Barter's Hill, directly across the street from Lars'. Downey's confectionary was east of this.

At the end of the street was J. D. Snow's, a favourite spot of Dickie's and mine. J. D. was a mild-mannered, soft-spoken, elderly gentleman. Dickie and I used to go there regularly to buy and trade comic books and magazines. His store had everything that one could imagine. I can still see J. D. leaning against one of the posts in his store, smoking his pipe and bartering with us; he always gave us a fair price. His store closed in the late '60s.

We used to go to Harris's barbershop at the end of

every month for our regular brush cut, which cost fifty cents. The more hair they took off, the longer you could go between haircuts. Dad would always drop by Harris's for a haircut or just a chat on his way to CN on Water Street. Harris's was a gathering place for the older people, like Jack Kidney's on Brazil Square; Dad and other men met there to discuss the news of the day.

****

These days, when I drive in downtown St. John's and pass by the places where those homes and businesses once stood, I always think about the wonderful times that I had there. I often stop the car by the corner of Brazil Street and Casey, where our corner used to be. The corner and Fossie Furlong's store are long gone, but I can visualize all us corner boys and girls standing there talking about everything under the sun and moon. No era of my life has ever been as special, as peaceful and innocent and enjoyable, as that time fifty years ago. I can still see Brazil Square bustling with people from out of town, many of them in St. John's for the very first time, full of excitement and enthusiasm, ready to take on the world. When I look over at John Street, I see the people who lived there, long gone now, walking home from buying groceries or running errands. I see people going into Walsh's Bakery on Central Street and leaving with their "scraps" or whatever they could afford to buy with what little money they had.

As I look back at those days, I see in my mind what I miss so much. People walking up Brazil Street, carrying their stainless steel lunch pails home from work at the dockyards or CN or some other downtown workplace, with contented faces after doing a hard day's work. It seems to me that back then people were happy with what they had, not unhappy with what they didn't have. They were full of energy from hard work. They were kind people who were always willing to lend a hand to those who had less than they did. They lived by life's rules and by God's.

making our own fun

We had none of the things that today's kids have, so we had to invent ways of enjoying ourselves. And so we were fond of practical jokes and good clean fun. A good many of us ended up on the butt end of a practical joke at one time or another. We were game for anything, and we thought nothing of bending the rules a little bit. We even thought stealing was perfectly innocent, if it involved something to eat.

In the early 1960s there were three main bakeries in St. John's: Walsh's on Central Street, Mammy's on Alexander Street, and Our Own on Water Street.

We used to go to Walsh's Bakery, just around the corner, to buy bread and scraps (the ends of pastries such as raisin squares and cakes, either left over or slightly marred in the baking process) for fifty cents a bag. It took us a few days' work to raise the money needed for these delicacies. The bags were usually full to the top, and it was a wonderful thing when we could afford them.

One day Dickie and I were on our way over to

Walsh's to buy some scraps when we ran into Willy, a school friend. He said he had just been at the bakery after buying three full boxes of bread (each containing twenty-four loaves), which were now stacked by the bakery's front door. Willy's uncle owned a large grocery store on George Street, and so we thought he had bought the bread for his uncle. (We should have realized that his uncle would have picked the boxes up himself. We found out later that they were by the door of the bakery because the delivery truck was going to pick them up.)

Willy went back to the bakery with us and came out of the office waving a bill of sale. He asked us to help him bring the bread to his house, which was just around the corner. He said he would give us a few loaves to take home. Dickie and I put a box each on our shoulders, and away we went.

When we got to Willy's house, he showed us the sales slip: he had paid for only one box of bread. He had gotten us to carry the two stolen ones home for him. We were so shocked that we hid the bread in his clubhouse, which was built onto the back steps in his garden. We raised the price of our little hijacking to half a dozen loaves each, threatening to tell his parents that he had made us accessories to his crime if he didn't give us what we wanted. Willy agreed. Later he sold the bread to some store for twenty-five cents a loaf, making a huge profit off what we took ("borrowed") for him. Good old Willy, he was a real salesman!

One night Dickie and I decided to have a look around inside Walsh's Bakery. Naturally, we were curious about such things as how they got all the raisins inside raisin squares, and how doughnuts were made. Of course, we took our tour after the bakery was closed.

We had gotten the idea of looking around after-hours about a month before, when we were at Walsh's buying bread and scraps. We told a worker we were doing a survey for school, which had to include information about what a bakery made and how they packaged and sold their products. We asked if he would show us around. He fell for it.

We had never seen the inside of a bakery. We were "wowed" when we were shown how things were made and what they were made from. We were even given a few treats. That did it. Two weeks later we made our return visit, hoping that they had forgotten we had been there, or at least who we were. We had no fear at all of getting caught. For us, it was just another way to have fun. The idea that it was illegal never entered our minds.

We entered by a door in the loft. We had gotten two old ladders and nailed them together to make one good one. After much climbing we reached the door, and pushed it hard enough to break the latch. Once we were inside, we started eating everything in sight. It was like Christmas all over again, but we were giving ourselves all the gifts. We ate until we were full: raisin squares, sinkers (pastries with a fudge filling that was like chocolate cake; two were the equivalent of a full meal, hence the name), and Dutch Creams (small, hollowed-out pastries filled with lemon and cream).

After about thirty minutes, we decided to make our getaway. We folded and taped two boxes and filled them with goodies. We also took two large plastic bags of raisins weighing about twenty pounds each (raisins were luxury items to us). We went out through the front door, walked home without a care in the world, and hid our bounty in the clubhouse.

I asked Dickie if he had closed and locked the bakery door behind him. "I thought that you did," he said. I told him I hadn't, and he said I should go back and lock it. I said there was no way I was going back after what we just did. We argued about it for a few minutes, and I got so frustrated that I walked back to lock up. I didn't realize that if the police came around the corner, not only would I be caught red-handed, I would also be the laughingstock of the street for getting caught. Talk about being naïve.

It took us a week to eat our goodies, and no one was the wiser. The raisins lasted longer; we ate them for weeks. That first night, after filling our stomachs again, we talked about Orphan Lake. We thought that this was what it must be like. If so, it was definitely where we wanted to be.

We did notice that when we decided to "tour" the bakery again a week later, all the windows had iron bars. I guess the absence of the food that we ate (about half of what was in Walsh's Bakery) had alerted them that someone had entered illegally.

We never meant to do any harm to anybody, or to damage anyone's property. We just didn't realize at the time that most of our pranks weren't strictly legal.

One day Dickie and I "borrowed" a bike. We were going down Springdale Street by Pike's Cycle Shop and noticed a brand new bike standing in front of the store.

Being the devils we were, we decided to take it for a spin.

It was a beautiful summer's day, with temperatures in the high eighties, and we decided to head to Bowring Park, approximately three miles away. We had ourselves a fine time riding our new prize. After about four hours, we decided to return the bike to the store. When we got back from the park, a friend told us that a bike had been stolen from Pike's and that the father of the boy who owned it was offering a $5 reward to anyone who returned the $200 gift he had given his son for his birthday—no questions asked.

We found out who the father was and phoned him. We said that we had tracked down the people who had stolen his son's bike (the dirty bastards), and after a struggle with the thieves we had manage to retrieve the bike. We then took it to Waterford Bridge Road (a rich area of town), where the family lived, and after many congratulations and thank yous we collected the reward for a bike that we had stolen in the first place. We couldn't believe our luck! What a great day for two little bicycle thieves.

Every time that I think of getting into mischief at that age I think about poor Marie Taylor. Marie was the daughter of Mike Taylor, who lived above the store on the corner. We didn't mean to treat her badly, but young boys are young boys, and one of their favourite things is to pick out one sweet little young lady to tease. Poor Marie was always our target.

I can see her now, wearing the new long, pink coat with big black buttons that her parents had bought for her. Miss Prim-and-Proper! She was always making sure we knew she had things, and that we didn't—at least that's the way it seemed to us. We knew that coat was an expensive one.

One day she left it in a closet while we were at a birthday party for one of our friends. Dickie and I decided to take all the buttons off the coat with a knife and hide them in our clubhouse. Well, you can guess what happened when Marie was getting ready to go home and she discovered that her buttons were missing. Naturally, we searched the house like everyone else, vowing to be heroes and return the buttons to the heroine as soon as they were found. But we were undone by our own pride: someone at the party had heard us boasting about our triumph, and squealed on us. We had to return the buttons, and we received a good tongue-lashing from our parents. We also had to pay $2 to Marie's dad for repairs to the coat, because we had ripped it when we took the buttons off. It killed us to part with $2 from our savings: we figured it probably meant $1 for coat repairs and $1 for Marie. We never did find out who squealed on us, lucky for them.

We used to skate on the sidewalk in front of our house; it was a great place to skate, since the street ran downhill. One night I was skating by myself and enjoying the solitude. Marie came along and started skating in what I considered to be my space. I asked her to leave several times, but she refused. It was just as much her sidewalk as it was mine, she said. Well, I wasn't having that, so the next time she passed me, I gave her a gentle push, hoping it would make her leave. But the push wasn't as gentle as I had intended. Marie left the sidewalk and sailed in through the front window of our house. My brother Calvin, who had been sitting in the chair in the living room where Marie landed, had just gotten up to go to the kitchen.

Marie, in slow motion, moving through the air, and the window glass breaking and flying everywhere, will forever be in my memory. I can also see me going, as fast as my young legs and my skates would carry me, up Brazil Street, trying to escape my fate. I was gone like a flash, the fastest disappearing act in history!

I hid out in a garden up the street for hours, without a hat or gloves to keep me warm. I nearly froze to death. I can still hear Dad calling to me to come home while I shivered in that garden a few hundred feet away. I kept looking at the house, at the window with cardboard in it instead of glass, and listening to Dad say he wasn't going to kill me, no matter how angry he sounded.

When I couldn't take the cold any longer, I headed next door to Dickie's and stayed there for the night. Dad gave me the bawling out of my life when I went home the next day. I lost my allowance (Dad was giving us fifty cents a week at one point, after he received a raise) for a month to pay for the window.

Luckily, Marie never got a scratch. To this day I still wonder why I didn't get a beating, or at least a crack on the backside, for what I did. I was very surprised at how calm Dad was; I could never figure that one out. I guess Mom had a say in the matter. She must have told him it was just an accident. Me, I knew better.

Marie's father, Mike Taylor, always gave me a dirty look every time I passed his house, but I had learned my lesson. After the window incident, Dickie and I left her alone. Some years later we heard that beautiful Marie had died, in Ontario, where her father had gone to find work.

One of our favourite pastimes was going to Bowring Park. The park land was donated to the city in 1911 by the Bowrings, one of the most prominent merchant families of St. John's. We practically lived in the park from seven until seventeen. We were there every weekend during the school year, and almost every day during the summer holidays. For Dickie and me, adventure was everywhere we turned when we visited the park. We loved going there. To us, it was as close to our Orphan Lake as we could get. When we were young children, Mom and Dad and my brothers and I often went to Bowring Park on Sunday. I don't remember how we got there—I'm guessing it was by bus—but I do remember it was an enjoyable family experience.

Just inside the park's main entrance, on the left-hand side, there is a small lake that used to offer boat rides. A person would take four to six people at a time in a small dory for a ten-minute ride. We looked forward to these rides, and we always made sure there were a few girls who were younger than we were in the boat before we got in, so we could tell them stories—about people who had drowned in the pond after their boat overturned. It used to frighten the hell out of them. (After a while, they wouldn't let us ride with other people.)

One day, on a fifty-cent dare, I stripped down to my swimming trunks and swam across the lake. This was strictly forbidden, because the lake was full of ducks and swans. I scared the hell out of them, not to mention the people in the boats. When I got to the other side after my ten minutes of fame, I was hauled out of the lake by a park employee and taken to see one of the park supervisors. He took my name, gave me a sharp lecture, and swore my parents would know all about the episode by the time I arrived home.

Every time we got into trouble, I was always amazed that everyone in St. John's seemed to know my parents and where they lived. And sure enough, my dad and Dickie's father were waiting for us with scowls on their faces when we got home. Our parents banned us from the park for a month. To two young mischief-makers in search of the kind of adventure only Bowring Park could provide, it was sheer misery.

We loved playing around the statue of Peter Pan, which was cast from the mould of the original Peter Pan statue in Kensington Gardens, London. It was commissioned by Sir Edgar R. Bowring, whose four-year-old granddaughter, Betty Munn, died when the SS *Florizel* sank on February 23, 1918 (my birthday, thirty-one years later). John Munn, her father and the managing director of Bowring Brothers, perished with her. The statue was unveiled on August 29, 1925, and has an inscription which reads "In memory of a little girl who loved the Park." We spent many days playing around the statue, envisioning ourselves as heroes or pirates, fighting the bad one-eyed captains and saving the damsels in distress.

After the damsels were safe, we would visit the Bungalow, which is in the heart of the park. Situated just down from the swimming pool, it had a canteen in those days, and a trip to the park wouldn't be complete without one of its custard cones. The lawns of the park are immaculately kept, and the grounds in front of the Bungalow are no exception. Trees line both sides of the Bungalow, many of which were planted by visiting dignitaries, such as Queen Elizabeth.

When we weren't up to some kind of devilment, we spent our time going to the movies. In our day, movies were only a dime. For a quarter (a lot of money in those days) we could get into the movies and also buy a soft drink and four or five one-cent bags of chips—potato chip scraps—along the way, to take into the theatre with us. Dickie and I loved the movies, and we went whenever we could afford it. We would go at least once a week.

The very first movie that I can remember seeing was at the York, which was a short distance west of the old post office on Water Street. The movie starred Bela Lugosi, and I think it was called *The Ape Man*. I can still see the ape climbing the side of a building on a drainpipe, and entering the bedroom of a woman, who screamed at the top of her lungs before she fainted. The ape climbed back down the outside of the building with the woman in tow. The movie scared the crap out of me. I had trouble sleeping for about a month, and I kept checking my window at night to make sure an ape wasn't climbing into it.

Some of the other movies theatres in St. John's were the Nickel, across from the Basilica on Harvey Road; the Cornwall, on Cornwall Avenue; and the Majestic, on the corner of Queen's Road and Duckworth Street. The Cornwall didn't show very good movies, so we usually went to the Nickel, the York, or the Majestic, which were closer to home anyway.

I think the first movie I saw at the Capitol on Henry Street was *Ben-Hur*, starring Charlton Heston. I remember waiting about five days to get tickets to see the 1974 movie *Earthquake* at the Capitol. It was the first movie to feature Sensurround, an audio feature that made you feel as though you were actually experiencing the quake. For us, it was fantastic and scary; we were frightened to death. All you could hear was oohs and aahs and girls screaming. Buildings fell and cars toppled over; people were crushed to death. What a movie! Lorne Greene of *Bonanza* fame was one of the main actors.

The Paramount Theatre on Harvey Road was beautiful inside and out. The architecture was art deco. Unfortunately, it was torn down in the '70s and replaced with an ugly office building some people call "little Atlantic Place" (after Atlantic Place on Water Street, a larger, uglier building). Watching movies at the Paramount had two advantages. It led us into another world, where we lost the hard realities of life and our imaginations could soar. And the Paramount was a place where we could hide from some of the trouble we managed to get into, where we could wait for things to cool down.

It was at the Paramount that Dickie and I discovered that alcohol and movie theatres do not really mix. I was about sixteen or seventeen at the time, and Dickie and I had just made a bit of money tearing down an old fence for some guy. We decided to spend some of it on *The Good, the Bad and the Ugly*, starring Clint Eastwood, Eli Wallach, and Lee Van Cleef. Dickie and I had been dying to see it. Clint Eastwood was the movie hero of the day, and, naturally, our idol. In those days cowboys were the tough guys, and they ruled the big and small screens. *Bonanza, Have Gun Will Travel, The Rebel,* and *Gunsmoke* were TV shows whose actors became our instant heroes.

The name of *our* movie could have been *The Good, the Bad and the Stupid*. On our way to watch the western, we decided to drop into a well-known bootlegger's on Cabot Street to see if we could take a message or do a delivery for him and make a few extra dollars. Nearly everyone went to bootleggers in those days, and many people had their liquor delivered to them. When we left the bootlegger's that Saturday, a "drop of stuff" happened to be sitting in the hallway, and somehow it found its way inside my coat and under my shirt. The bootlegger was worried about using us as delivery boys. Not being sure of our age, he instructed us to go through back gardens, and to say, if we got caught with the bottle, that we had stolen the liquor from someone. He had no idea I had another bottle hidden inside my shirt.

We had already experimented with having a few beers, but hard liquor was something we knew nothing about. To us booze was booze—we didn't realize there was a difference between rum and beer. We had tried to get some of the sudsy stuff, but our friend was all out, so we decided the rum would do. We arrived at the Paramount a half an hour before the movie started, to have a bite to eat. Then we bought two large soft drinks and went to the washroom, where we poured some of the contents of the bottle of Screech into the drink containers. The first few drinks didn't seem to do us much harm, but about an hour or so later the rum started to hit us—we had pretty well finished the bottle by then. We started yelling at the top of our voices, telling Clint Eastwood to watch out for the bad guys sneaking up on him. A bridge exploded when Clint and Eli Wallach were in the water, and we nearly died. We thought that our hero was dead and gone, and that we would never see him again in another movie! We had to do something, so we gave Clint and Eli some encouragement: "Clint, what the Christ are you guys doing, you dummies? Get the fuck down or you are both going to die!" These were just a few of the messages we delivered to our onscreen heroes.

Several times the ushers came to the balcony and warned us to be quiet. That only made us worse, and we started harassing some young ladies in the next row, who also told us to be quiet. One can guess our drunken response.

Finally the ushers came back with the manager. Dickie had just thrown the empty liquor bottle at the screen because a Mexican guy was about to shoot our hero, Clint. We were grabbed by the scruff and evicted. I don't know why they didn't call the police. We were obviously in a very drunken state, and Fort Townshend, the police headquarters, was just around the corner from the theatre. Lucky for us they didn't: our fathers would have killed us for sure if we had been arrested.

Now we were two drunken young men struggling to walk up Harvey Road, and looking around to see what kind of fun we could have. Our first stop was Rice's Fish and Chips (now The Big R), where we consumed a large feed of fish and chips. We were soon asked to leave because of our uncontrollable laughing fits. We then headed down to Water Street and tried to get into some clubs, with no success. We walked—stumbled, mostly—around downtown St. John's, having no idea what time it was or what we were doing. Dickie and I could never remember exactly where we went that night. We lost the rest of the money we had in our pockets, about ten bucks, or perhaps we spent it in our drunken stupor.

Eventually, we ended up at Vera Buck's store on Monroe Street with a dozen bottles of beer that we had somehow gotten our hands on—probably "borrowed" from somewhere. (I have a vague recollection it was from my buddies at the Belmont Club.) We were about to find out that liquor and beer are a bad mix. We partied until supper, ended up on the corner, and then at the clubhouse, where we passed out. I can still see Dad and Blackie White in the pitch darkness of the night as they took us out and dragged us home. As soon as our fathers woke us, we both started to throw up. I thought I would never stop; I can't remember ever being as sick as I was that night. I was sure I was going to die.

Dad was good enough about it—just a few boots in the arse to wake me up. And he waited until the next evening when I got out of bed (still sick as a dog) to shout at me. Only for Mom saying to him, "Leave him be, Ned," I probably would have been killed. Dickie fared much the same: Blackie read him the riot act. We were lucky that neither of us in our drunken state had damaged anyone's property or gotten in a fight. Our dads surely would have disowned or killed us. We learned a valuable lesson that day about the dangers of alcohol, and one we would not soon forget. Why, it was all of a week before we drank again! I often wonder how we grew up without being skinned alive by our parents.

When we didn't have money for the movies, we sometimes went to *Art Andrews's Dance Party* at the CJON television station in Buckmaster's Circle. It was a local show, shot live, and a big hit. Kids danced to the latest music, and we all watched the show after school to see who was at the dance. It was a local craze. It was broadcast on CJON right before Don Jamieson and *News Cavalcade* came on at suppertime.

nhl hockey in newfoundland

Being proud Newfoundlanders and Canadians, we were always into the great local and national pastime of men of all ages: hockey. It was a big part of our lives. We all dreamed that we were the next Bobby Orr, Gordie Howe, Bobby Hull, and the rest of the NHL heroes of that era.

Television came to Newfoundland in 1955, but our family couldn't afford a set until 1958 or 1959. I can still see our first television. It was a big old clunker that was coin operated. You dropped a quarter into a slot and the television ran for approximately two to three hours. This was very irritating, because it would stop dead in the middle of a program, and someone would have to put another quarter in. We had it for about a year before Dad got another one, a second-hand RCA Victor.

In the early '60s, NHL hockey started broadcasting, in the middle of the second period. There were only six teams in the NHL back then. The Original Six consisted of the Montreal Canadiens, the Toronto Maple Leafs, the New York Rangers, the Detroit Red Wings, the Chicago Black Hawks, and the Boston Bruins. Many people my age are still dedicated to one of the Original Six. We all had a favourite team and a favourite player. My team has been the Detroit Red Wings since I was six; my heroes in those days were Alex Delvecchio and Gordie Howe. Dickie's team was the Chicago Black Hawks, and his hero was Bobby Hull. In those days you idolized your team, and you stayed with them whether they lost or won. At one point my Red Wings didn't make the playoffs for nearly ten years, but I stayed with them until they did.

Hockey was one of our most important winter pastimes. We spent many nights playing hockey in our back gardens until our parents called us in to go to bed.

Besides the NHL games and the back garden games, we went to Memorial Stadium, when we had the money, to watch local hockey games. High school hockey produced a lot of rivalry in those days. The Guards, St. Bon's, the Feildians, and St. Pat's provided us with the same kind of excitement we got from watching NHL games.

During the '60s we played mostly in two places, our back garden on Brazil Street and Harry Husk's garden on John Street. And play hockey we did. We visualized ourselves as hockey heroes, each of us scoring the winning goal in game seven of the Stanley Cup Final. We spent many long hours in both gardens playing the game we loved so much.

In our garden we had a little hill that curved up on a ten- to fifteen-degree incline, which made playing without losing the ball difficult. It would sometimes take off when it hit the bank, and we would have to hop the fence to retrieve it, which necessitated stopping the game. We decided to do something about it one summer. We spent most of the holidays digging up the bank and flattening the garden into a presentable hockey rink. We must have moved 200 wheelbarrows full of soil before we were able to make the surface level. Such was our dedication to hockey.

All my brothers and the guys from neighbouring streets played. Ed Sweeney was the best goalie, and nearly everyone wanted him on his team. The game was so popular with us that we not only had our own teams, but kept statistics for the games. We pretended we were the Boston Bruins playing the Toronto Maple Leafs, or the Detroit Red Wings playing the Montreal Canadiens. It always seemed natural that one of the teams would be Montreal or Toronto, and one of the others would be an American team. Initially, we played in pairs, two players against two other players. One team had a goalie and either a forward or a defenceman; the other team would have two rushing forwards. After a timed five-minute period, the teams switched—the other team would have the goalie and the forward or defenceman. After two five-minute periods, the team with the most goals won. Soon enough, when word got around that the game was on in our back garden, everyone in the neighbourhood and adjacent streets wanted in on the action.

When we had enough people, we would play three or four people on each team and the games would become very intense—our own NHL. Somehow there never seemed to be a shortage of people willing to play.

Sometimes when we played teams from other streets we would hold tournaments and make believe we were playing for the Stanley Cup. The odd time we would hold a tournament for money, when we had some. During these games we were the stars of our era: Bobby Orr and Bobby Hull, Terry Sawchuk, Johnny Bower, Jacques Plante. Sometimes we imagined we were Alex Faulkner, the first Newfoundlander to play in the NHL. When we were playing hockey, we were thrown into another world. We played for the right to be called the best in the league. There was never a major fight among us when we played. When you won you won, and when you lost you didn't complain.

We used to make money from a homemade hockey game, an idea we picked up from Fozzie Furlong. The game was easy. You took a sheet of paper and divided it into one hundred squares. On the top you wrote "Away" and on the left-hand side of the paper you wrote "Home." People paid a dime apiece to put their names in the squares on the sheet. When all one hundred squares were filled out, someone, with another person as a witness, would draw numbers (from one to ten) out of a hat and put them on the sheet diagonally and across the top. This would give each person who purchased a square a final score for both teams competing in Saturday night's NHL game. Whoever got the correct score would win $5, and the seller got the other $5. Dickie and I often used this game during our teenage years to make a quick buck.

"The NHL in Newfoundland," as we called it, was a big neighbourhood bond, and it also united us with other boys from different areas of the city who came to play. Our back garden on Brazil Street became a hockey mecca, and all personal and territorial barriers came down when we played hockey. We were the NHL heroes of our day, and that was all that mattered to us.

I often think about our hockey games when I pass our old house. I can still picture Dickie and me out in the back garden on the ice on a winter's night, with the snow falling and the stars shining in the heavens. Or sitting down in the corner of the yard by the old oil tank after the games, talking about the future and what it would hold for us. Talking about finding Orphan Lake, possibly when we were drafted by the NHL.

Although we never did make the NHL, hockey certainly gave us a good grasp of unity and discipline.

the assassination of jfk

The assassination of President Kennedy was a huge event for us, as it was for most people on that sad day in 1963. I remember that day as if it were yesterday.

I was fourteen years old, walking home from Holy Cross School on Patrick Street when I heard the news. As I turned the corner of Hamilton Avenue and Patrick Street, another Holy Cross student told me that JFK had been shot and killed by a sniper in Dallas. I stood there dumbfounded. We had just been talking about him in school that day. I thought it meant the end of the world. Working-class people in St. John's in those days had very little knowledge of the rest of the world. Everyone I knew thought the Communists were responsible for killing the American president; they were the bad guys of that era. People talked about them ruling the world, taking over the schools, churches, and the government. Everyone knew that it was only a matter of time. They were everywhere, even in Newfoundland. They were waiting to take over the province! This paranoia was fuelled by the Cuban Missile Crisis in 1962;

people thought that Castro had had Kennedy killed. Of course, there are still many theories about what happened on November 22, 1963.

I ran home from school frightened to death. What did this catastrophe mean for my family and my friends? I felt that my parents would set me straight. When I got home, there were people standing in the streets outside their houses. And Mom and Dad had no real answers for me. Surely the world had gone completely mad. I can still see my folks sitting in front of the radio waiting to hear about the fate of the world. They believed that another war was about to start. Within the next few days, our fears were put to rest. Apparently Lee Harvey Oswald had been acting on his own.

As kids, we used to go to Fort Pepperrell, an American base in the east end of St. John's. The Americans built several bases in Newfoundland in 1941. The province was considered strategic, situated as it was between North America and Europe. Dickie and I went to Fort Pepperrell the day after JFK's assassination to see what the soldiers were thinking about it all.

I remember a Sergeant Randell (we never knew his first name) who used to give us food and really did some nice things for us when we went there to do chores for them. He always seemed to know that we, being from the poorer section of St. John's, did not have very much in the way of food or clothing, so this guy was always good to us and we liked him and treated him with respect. That was one thing we really liked about the American soldiers. They always treated us nicely when we visited.

He looked at us, then stared at the American flag, which was at half-mast, and told us that a great man had just been shot and that 1963 and the assassination would be remembered forever in history. The whole base was silent. He said that no one would ever forget where they were the day President Kennedy was shot.

The Americans left Pepperrell in August, 1961. The troops moved out, and the base was officially handed over to Canada and Newfoundland. The American flag was taken down in a ceremony, but a few soldiers stayed on.

holy cross

I attended Holy Cross from 1955 to 1965, when I went to Brother Rice on Bonaventure Avenue. Holy Cross was established by the Christian Brothers. It opened its doors on September 9, 1890. Back in those days it was only a four-room school. It was expanded in 1914, with the addition of several new classrooms and a small recreational area. In 1946, a new sixteen-room school with a modern gymnasium was opened on the same site.

Holy Cross was destroyed by a dreadful fire on December 11, 1969. I was there, and saw it burn to the ground. It was a sad thing to see the school I loved reduced to ashes. There was a rumour of arson, but nothing came of it.

I can still remember Holy Cross with great clarity. I can stand in its dark, polished hallways and walk through them, floor by floor. I hear boys chatting, and the echoes of others shouting and playing, waiting for the ringing of the school bell to call them to class. I hear teachers reprimanding boys for being late, and shrill voices laughing and singing. I hear the sound silence made when you walked alone through the hallways late in the afternoon.

The gymnasium was down a flight of steps from the second floor. I can still see boys playing basketball or throwing a volleyball, and the shine that the polished floors always had. Underneath the gym was a bowling alley, where many great bowlers got their start. Holy Cross produced many fine hockey players and soccer players. Some of those from my day were Fox and Farmer Reddy, and Butch and Frank Reddy. Many young men became fine athletes during the years they spent there. We had wonderful sports days every year, when we dressed in our best school clothes (white shirt, grey pants, red and gold cap). It was something we all looked forward to. Excitement was at its peak on that day. We were given a dollar or two by our parents to spend on games of chance for prizes. Captain Tom O'Grady taught us precision drills, which we showed off to parents and visitors and former students.

Dickie and I were no great athletes, but you couldn't beat us at the sport of practical joking. One day we went in to the basketball locker room and switched the teams' clothes and socks around, so that they would have a hard time finding who owned what when game time rolled around. Then we put their sneakers in different lockers, so that one player would have a size six and a size seven sneaker and another would have an eight and a ten. Another time we taped a pair of shorts to one basketball net and a jockstrap to another before a game with Brother Rice.

We would do anything for a laugh. We were not bad kids, but we weren't angels either. One of the jocks on the basketball team snubbed us one evening at a

Holy Cross dance. We got even by taking the clothes out of his locker and throwing them out a back window. I can still see his shorts, socks, and gold and red Holy Cross sweater blowing in the wind in the trees behind the school.

Holy Cross bingo nights are still vivid in my memory. I used to change bingo cards for people trying to win a couple of dollars to supplement their meagre incomes. We made very little money in bingo tips in those days. We didn't realize that the prize money was needed to help support families of six to maybe a dozen people. If you received any money at all for being a card changer, you were in heaven as you thought about how you would spend your newly acquired fortune all the way home. One night a lady who had won a game gave me a dollar for changing her cards. I went home on cloud nine! However, it was difficult to make it home with your wealth. Usually it was spent at Power's or Marty's or on one of Lars' custard cones.

Many of the boys I went to school with at Holy Cross are still good friends. Some of my former classmates include such characters and great men as Johnny Doyle, Martin "Marty" Burton, Kevin and Bobby Corbett, Brian Power, Tom Prim, Duper and Clem Hayward, Bobby Forristall, Maurice and Dave Smith, Paul Stead, Tommy Connors, Robert Kennedy, Mike Yetman, Hayward Pike, Damian Hayes, Ted Doyle, Chris Murphy, Charlie Furey, Dave and Ed Luby, Nana Murphy, Howie and Chinny Vedd, Bill and Ronnie Abbott, Bobby Constantine, Gary and Derm Duggan, Mike Browne, Bren O'Brien, Joe Wadden, Gary Philpott, and Leonard Edison. There were many, many others—good, honest, hard-working young men who became fine members of the community.

I was taught by some great Irish Christian Brothers and lay teachers who were instrumental in instilling values into us. They made sure we had what we needed for the world we would encounter on the day we left the school behind. Good, kind-hearted Brothers such as John Buckingham, John Rivers, Harry French, and Kevin Veitch, and so many others who worked hard to ensure that our future would be a bright one. And terrific lay teachers such as Frank Galgay—a remarkable man who is still a good friend—Bill Connolly, Mike McCarthy, and Pat Leonard. They were men of vision and dedication.

I was a member of the Holy Cross Tap Dancers for a few years. In those days, a lot of work was put into our concerts. They were always staged to a full gymnasium. Not many people owned a television set or drove a car, and going out was expensive, so concerts such as ours were a big draw. People walked for miles just to enjoy them.

After I had been a dancer for a few years, the Holy Cross tumbling team caught my eye. I was shy about joining, but friends of mine, Ted Doyle and Tommy Dodd, convinced me to do it. I couldn't make the hockey or soccer teams; most of those guys were way ahead of me in ability and agility. But tumbling was just right for me. I ended up loving it and living for it. It seemed to be what I had been born to do. The years that I was on the team were some of the happiest of my school life.

I met my first real girlfriend when I was at Holy

Cross, a young lady who went to St. Patrick's School. Mary Doyle was sweet and easygoing, and I was awed by her beauty. I saw her nearly every day after school. We "dated" for about a year. I remember seeing my first colour television set at her brother Ray's house, in 1962. Ray, his wife, Maureen, and I sat and watched Ray's favourite team, the Montreal Canadiens, play the Boston Bruins. I can't remember who won. I was too busy being amazed by the TV.

the beating

Many former students that I run into from my Holy Cross days speak fondly about the school. Why wouldn't they? It was a beautiful school, and we had a lot of good times there. But for me, the good will always be tainted by the evil of abuse that came from some of those in authority. I try to expel these "men" from my mind, but their psychological and emotional legacy is not so easily dismissed.

By the time I was attending Holy Cross, some of the Irish Christian Brothers had strayed a long way from the path of holy living. Brothers who regularly used me and others as punching bags, and worse. I used to think of them as the Dark Ones (and that was a long time before *Star Wars* was filmed). In those days, people in authority had absolute control, and not all of them were fit to wield it. But society had given it to them: our parents were uneducated and naive and held the Roman Catholic Church in great esteem. Many a student received a beating at home when their parents found out that a Brother or a nun had been disobeyed. But family beatings were nothing compared to the abuse some of us suffered in school. And we had no one to turn to—our parents and the police were part of the problem back then, not the solution. We had our friends to talk to; our God-loving parents were as afraid of Church authorities as we were.

Society was different in those days. It was more tightly structured. There were lots of rules for behaviour, and discipline was strict. This wasn't so bad in general, but it was a living nightmare when psychologically damaged people were in control of you. I first found out about Holy Cross discipline at the age of five when I spent my school fee money on fudge, chips, and soft drinks at Power's store. When a kid from a poorer section of town had a dollar in those days, it wasn't going to the school for fees. At least mine wasn't. The next day, after my father and mother had scolded me for doing what I did, a Christian Brother also scolded me—and hit me on the side of the head several times. Not lightly, either. I learned to put up with being hit and strapped; I wasn't a bad child or unruly—no worse than most—but I became one of the favourite targets of some of the Brothers anyway. I couldn't understand why I was always selected for "discipline" and other kids weren't. I guess the Brothers knew I could endure the physical aspect of a beating. They also knew who to pick on. I was small and poor. But the more they hit me, the more stubborn I became. I guess that came from my dad, who wouldn't let anyone push him around.

Several years after that first Brother cuffed me, I was beaten severely.

It was the spring of 1959. I was ten years old, and a member of the Holy Cross Tap Dancers. I had just finished a dancing lesson one afternoon and was ready to head home when a certain Brother asked me to stay behind for "a chat." I can still remember how nice he was in front of the other boys when he asked me to remain after practice. I had no idea what he wanted me for, but I soon found out. The real lesson he wanted to teach me had nothing to do with dancing.

After the rest of the boys had gone home, Brother Dave (not his real name) levelled a barrage of accusations at me. Suddenly I was being pushed up against the wall in a closet. When I asked him why he was doing this to me, he used a serious curse word. That really startled me. It was the first time I had ever heard a Brother curse. Cops swore all the time, but a member of a religious order? Never.

"You saucy, ungrateful little fucker!" he said. "Don't you dare ask me any more stupid questions. I'm the one that asks the questions around here. I can see that you have no respect for authority."

Now, it took a lot to make me afraid of someone. Dickie and I were often in fights, and I had been knocked around and strapped by other Brothers without so much as a whimper escaping my lips. But that day I was terrified: I knew I was about to experience something outside the range of the usual disciplinary experience. I actually thought that he was going to kill me. I saw pure, icy hatred in his eyes, and heard crazy anger in his voice. What happened to me that day should never have happened to me or to any other boy. Brother Dave looked at me as if I were a small animal he had cornered and was about to finish off. It was as if he had been waiting all his life for a moment like this to present itself so he could purge himself of whatever demons he was harbouring. His first swing hit me square in the mouth, and I could feel it swell as soon as he connected.

He pushed me up against the wall again. I told him to stop, to think about what he was doing. I tried to fight him off. I made the mistake of pushing him, hard, to try to get him away from me. I guess I pushed the bastard a little bit too hard. He tripped in a coat that was lying on the floor and stumbled. He fell against the wall and caught his shoulder on a coat hook, which made him grimace in pain. I was thinking at the time that if I pushed him away, it would force him to rethink what he was about to do to me. But then he came at me with a vengeance.

I tried to protect myself, but he was about 170 pounds and I was only seventy. I never had time to be afraid: he rained blow upon blow on my shoulders and head, screaming at me the whole time. Then he left the closet and came back with a yardstick. I knew I was really in for it then. I would like to think that he did what he did because I had pushed him, but I realized later it was just pure hatred, the source of which I will never know.

He accused me of so many things that I can't even remember what they all were. Stealing, cursing, fighting—you name it. In his mind I was the arch-devil of the entire school. And I knew I wasn't; I knew I hadn't done half the things he was accusing me of. He said that he had been watching me for years, and now it was time for him as the person in authority to "change your ways and set you straight." There was no one there to help me, or even witness the beating that began then.

I believe most people have a mean streak—small or large—hidden inside them, and most of us have a few skeletons in our closets. Some mean streaks and skeletons stay hidden forever, but sometimes people hit that crazy moment in their lives, and then it all comes tumbling out. I think that was the crazy moment for him.

He pushed me, hit me, and jammed me up against the wall, laying several short, powerful blows at my midsection and upper body. He slapped me in the head and around the arms and shoulders, shouting at me the entire time. Finally, I couldn't take it anymore. I cursed at him, telling him not to fucking touch me any more or I would make sure that he never hurt another boy again. I remember wishing Dickie were there: we could have inflicted some damage together.

Did that stop him? No, it only made him angrier. He put me in a headlock, bent me across his knee, and started hitting me with the yardstick on the backside and legs. If I counted twenty whacks, I counted forty. Blow after blow, smack after smack. All I could think of was what I would do to him when I was old enough to fight back. He beat me so hard and for so long that he was exhausted and breathless when he finished. His face was bright red—I remember hoping he would have a heart attack. Then he told me to get out of his sight and warned me not to tell anyone about what he had done, or he would do it again. I will never forget how he smelled. His clothes had that just-washed scent of fresh sheets. I associate that odour with him to this day.

I was so sore that it took me an hour to get home from school, a fifteen-minute walk. I thought that if he hadn't stopped hitting me he might have killed me. I thought about all the fights Dickie and I had been in, and how I could never have imagined that level of violence. Or hatred. I had never seen hatred like that before.

A little part of me thought that maybe I deserved it. If Mom and Dad found out, how would I explain it? My legs, back, and shoulders were bloody. I had a swollen jaw. I remember thinking that I would have to make up a whopper of a lie to tell my parents. (Remember, those were the days of total power for those in authority, and their authority was never questioned by good Catholics.) In the end I decided not to tell them. When I got home I told my mother that I wasn't hungry. I was very tired, I said, and was going to bed. She knew that it wasn't like me. I tried to avoid her eyes, but mothers have a keen sense when it comes to their children. She asked me if I had been in another fight. I said yes and that I just wanted to go to bed and forget about what had happened. I can still see her looking at me in the hallway. I turned away so that she wouldn't see how beaten up I was. (She wore glasses, and I was hoping her eyesight was so poor that she couldn't see my wounds.) I went upstairs to the bathroom and put some rubbing alcohol on the cuts and bruises, and then I went to bed, aching all over. I fell into a deep sleep in a matter of minutes.

My father came home after supper, and Mom told him that I had acted very strangely when I got home from school. She had checked on me while I slept, and had seen the cuts and bruises. My father came upstairs and woke me from my tossing sleep. He asked me if I could get up and stand by the bed for him. I did, and he saw the state of my face, my legs, and my backside. And I saw the rage in his face—anger such as I never saw in him before or after.

No lies were going to work that day. He asked me what happened. I cried, and told him what Brother Dave had done to me in the clothes closet. He told me not to worry about it—it would never happen to me again. He asked me if I could walk. When I said yes, he told me to get my clothes on, because we were going up to the Holy Cross monastery to talk to Brother Dave and the principal, Brother Larry Angel.

Despite my father's rage, he had a calmness about him that I knew didn't bode well for Brother Dave or anyone else who got in his way. We walked to Holy Cross without exchanging one word. He carried me on his back when I found it difficult to walk.

When we got there, he made me stand by the steps of the monastery's entrance. He knocked on the door, and asked the Brother who answered to get Brother Dave; he told the Brother he wanted to speak with him. When Brother Dave came to the door, my father grabbed him and shook him violently, then pushed him up against the wall. Then my dad did something very uncharacteristic. He punched Brother Dave twice in the face, knocking him to the floor. He told Brother Dave and Brother Angel, who had arrived at the door by then, that if anyone ever touched me or another of his sons again, they would pay very dearly. Then he took me from my hiding place by the side of the steps and made me show Brother Angel my injuries.

Brother Dave denied everything—he called me a liar. Dad had to be held back from Brother Dave by Brother Angel. Brother Dave said that I had been fighting with another boy, which is how I had gotten the beating. That made my father really angry. He knew that a beating like that had not come from another boy. Dad said he didn't believe a word. He asked Brother Dave for the other boy's name, but there was no name, of course. Dad told them both that he would severely hurt anyone, Brother or not, who raised a hand to one of his sons again. He threatened to go to the police. Brother Angel took him aside and talked him out of it. I can still see him and Dad walking up the road beside the monastery. Brother Angel had his arm around my father's shoulder, and apparently he told my father he would take care of it, that he would mete out severe discipline to Brother Dave. Yeah, right.

My father brought up this incident to me many times. He always said that he had made a big mistake by not doing what he should have done: phone the police. But I was never more proud of my father than when he made that trek to the monastery on my behalf. Brother Dave wasn't at Holy Cross the next year; he had been transferred to another school, somewhere on the mainland, where he probably did the same thing to other kids. Years later, when I heard of his death, I had no pity. I have never wished any person harm, but I have never been able to forgive Brother Dave for what he did that day.

Dickie was very angry at Brother Dave for what he

had done to me, and he wanted both of us to go and beat him up. I told him to drop it. It was over and done with. Dickie didn't get the same treatment at school as many of us did, because he was so big. I guess the Brothers were afraid of what he might do if provoked.

Some of the Brothers used to put you out in the hallway if you were doing something wrong (or if they thought you were doing something wrong). Brother Angel patrolled the hallways, and he would ask why you were out there. After you told him, he would give you three or four smacks on each hand with a thick leather strap. The strap was between two and three feet long, and about two or three inches wide. It was the same kind of strap that hung on the side of a barber's chair. When it came down on your hand you damn well felt it. But you could never show that you were in pain; if you did, the other boys would treat you like a coward. We used to listen for whimpering when students were sent into the hallway. I always used to get a few extra on each hand because I refused to let the pain show on my face. I just took it in stride. You also got hit a few extra times if you pulled your hand away, or for any other reason they could think of, for that matter. If Brother Angel was in the mood, you got a couple on the backside for good measure.

Other Brothers would pick you up from your seat by putting their hands on your hair just above your ears and pulling you skyward. Did that ever hurt! It was worse than any strapping. No wonder we boys and girls rebelled against some of those teachers, Brothers, and nuns, who considered us lower class and deserving of ridicule and physical abuse.

The majority of the Christian Brothers were fine

people, as I have said. I don't know what was wrong with the others. I remember one student swearing that if a Brother ever hit him, he would hit him back. When it finally happened, he hit the Brother and walked out of school. He never came back. (Eventually, he ended up opening a store in town.)

One Remembrance Day our class had to learn the poem "In Flanders Fields." Try as I might, I could not master the words. I kept getting them mixed up. I had only two days to learn it because I had been ill and out of school. The other students had had a week to get it down pat. But you can imagine which student was picked to recite the poem. I did pretty well, making only a few small mistakes until I got to the last few lines, which I flubbed. The Brother made me write it out 200 times over that weekend, so I "would always remember and appreciate the finer points of a great poem." It's no wonder to this day that I know the poem off by heart. I recite it respectfully every year on Remembrance Day. Not all discipline was pointless.

Confession was an education in itself. We went to St. Patrick's Church, a short distance from the school, led from the school down the street and into the church in double file. Across the street was St. Patrick's Girls School, and, of course, they were led to confession on the opposite side of the street. Heaven forbid if you were to glance at, talk to, or make an off-the-cuff comment to the opposite sex. If you were caught, you could expect a slap on the side of the head or something more serious, depending on the offence. You had to be very careful about what you said to the girls on the other side of the street, and how you looked at them.

Boys sat on the right side of the church and girls on the left. We could whisper among ourselves, but communication with the opposite sex was not recommended unless you were extremely brave. If you had to talk with a young lady about something, the best way to do it was through a note, which would be passed hand to hand. You would fake your writing in case a Brother intercepted it. Even if the girl was your sister, you weren't allowed to talk to her.

Confession was a solemn affair. You did not go to it with a "serious sin" on your soul unless you were scared half to death first! There were venial sins—the minor ones, like using vulgar language, forgetting to say your prayers, white lies—and the dreaded mortal sin. These ranged from stealing and sex (including sex with yourself, or even a fairly innocent kiss with the opposite sex) to murder. If you were taking one of the latter to the confessional, you could be in for serious trouble, depending on which priest was hearing confession. We were afraid to tell a priest a mortal sin for fear that he would throw us out of the confessional in front of our friends. In which case we would not only be embarrassed, but excommunicated from God and the church and doomed to spend the remainder of eternity in hell. Therefore, any real sin you committed stayed with you. Many lads were shouted out of the confessional for telling the priest their sins.

I had so many sins on my soul, I knew that I would be cast into the furnaces of hell for two lifetimes if the priest in the confessional ever heard about them. It was no wonder that I stayed away from confessing my real sins until adulthood. You had to choose your words carefully in the confessional, or face the wrath of the priest. And God's wrath too, they told us.

One young boy quit going to church after Father Murphy threw him out of the confessional for confessing a "terrible" sin. He had kissed a girl the evening before, three or four times. The Roman Catholic Church and sex in any form have never had an easy relationship. Kissing a girl, and on a school night—heaven forbid! The boy had told us before he went to see the priest, and we told him to keep it quiet, but he didn't listen.

Forty years later the Hughes Inquiry would reveal the extent of the corruption of authority in the Roman Catholic Church. Brothers, priests, and others would be punished for the physical, sexual, and emotional abuse of children under their care. Brothers and priests I grew up with (such as Brother Edward English) were front and centre during the Hughes Inquiry. They deserved to be punished. I know many people who suffered from their abuse.

Not all of the accused were guilty, however. Brother John Buckingham was the son of the people who used to own Buckingham's hardware store at the bottom of Barter's Hill. He was a saint of a man if there ever was one. He taught me and my friends at Holy Cross, and we thought very highly of him. Two former students accused him of lewd acts, but we knew that gentle man couldn't have done anything even close to what his accusers had claimed. The two who accused him were later found guilty of perjury.

I have no pity for those who were guilty. I was one of the young men who suffered, although I am grateful

I wasn't sexually abused. The abuse of power, the constant and senseless beating of children who, like me, ended up with psychological scars, had to end some time. I am glad I was alive to see it. Though only a few Christian Brothers abused their power, even one was one too many. I have waited a long time to speak of what happened to me when I was a child. Perhaps now that child will find some peace.

photographs

LEFT: Mom standing on Monroe Street, circa 1945 (Author photo)
RIGHT: Malcolm "Dickie" White (Author photo)

Dickie and two buddies in a backyard in St. John's, circa 1965 (Courtesy of Mary White)

LEFT: Me, age eight, in 1957 (Author photo) RIGHT: Some of the Brazil Street crowd, circa 1957-58. I am at the bottom right and my brother Edward is at the top right (Author photo)

Brazil Square when it was being demolished in the 1980s (Author photo)

LEFT: Mom, my brothers, and I in Bowring Park, circa 1950s (Author photo) RIGHT: Mom and her brothers and sisters standing in front of our house during Come Home Year, 1966. L-R: Uncle Mac, Aunt Violet, Mom, Aunt Josephine, Aunt Patricia, and Uncle Angus (Author photo)

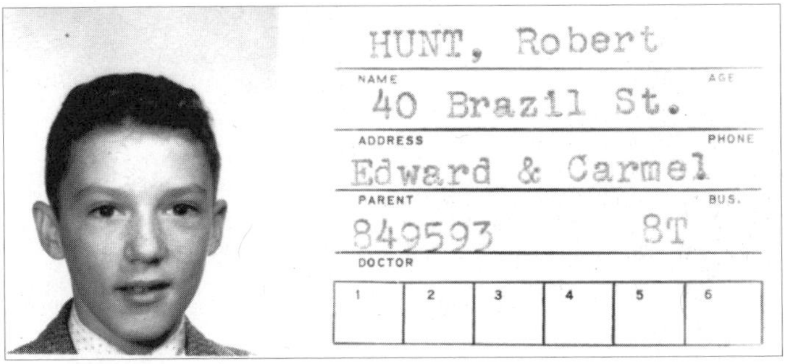

HUNT, Robert
NAME AGE
40 Brazil St.
ADDRESS PHONE
Edward & Carmel
PARENT BUS.
849593 8T
DOCTOR

1	2	3	4	5	6

Photo of me, age thirteen, in the Holy Cross school rolodex. This card survived the 1969 fire. (Author photo)

The Hunt boys, circa 1956 or 1957. L-R: Me, Edward, Angus, Hubert, and Calvin. (Author photo)

LEFT: Dickie and a friend on Holy Cross Sports Day, circa 1957 (Courtesy of Mary White) RIGHT: Four of us in Maher's, circa 1957. L-R: Hubert, Calvin, me, and Edward (Author photo)

Dad with one of his friends, circa 1940. His friend later lost his life when their ship was torpedoed during World War II. (Author photo)

The old Paramount Theatre shortly before it was demolished (Courtesy of *The Evening Telegram*)

LEFT: Dad holding me, 1949 (Author photo) RIGHT: Mom and me in Bowring Park, circa 1956 (Author photo)

Dickie White's family. BACK ROW: Davis, Mary (Dickie's mother), Ed Martin with wife Laura and new baby, and Louise. FRONT ROW: Darlene, and Dickie (Courtesy of Mary White)

LEFT: My older brother Edward and me in Bowring Park, with Dad in the background, 1958 (Author photo) RIGHT: The Arcade on Water Street (Courtesy of Harry Husk)

Dad, second from left, while working with Canadian National Railways, circa 1952 (Author photo)

Old houses on Barron Street, off of Casey Street
(Courtesy of Harry Husk)

The old *Daily News* building on Duckworth Street
(Courtesy of *The Evening Telegram*)

Bowring Park Bungalow
(Courtesy of the City of St. John's Archives, 05-07-025)

Holy Cross Tumbling Team, circa 1960. I am on the right, wearing sweater. In back is Brother Kevin Vietch. (Author photo)

The old Bowring Park swimming pool
(Courtesy of the City of St. Johns Archives, 19-03-047)

CN's *Caribou*, nicknamed the "Newfie Bullet," circa 1950s
(Author photo)

White's Fish & Chips store, corner of Casey and Brazil Square (Author photo)

LEFT: Mom, age twenty, in her home of Port Royal, a resettled community, in 1938 (Author photo) RIGHT: The Belmont Lounge, 1965 (Courtesy of the City of St. John's Archives, 11-03-032)

LEFT: Mom and Dad's wedding, 1940 (Author photo)
RIGHT: Ed and me in Bowring Park, circa 1950s (Author photo)

Dad with a group ready to go overseas, circa 1940s. He is second down from top right. (Author photo)

Holy Cross School, 1968
(Courtesy of the City of St. John's Archives, 02-04-003)

The London, New York & Paris on Water Street
(Courtesy of the City of St. John's Archives, 26-0-016)

Dickie White, circa 1977. Paddy Flynn's store is in the background.
(Courtesy of Mary White)

Dickie White, circa 1985
(Courtesy of Mary White)

the ghost of tessier's lane

When we were young boys, we used to wonder about ghosts. Did they really exist? Not that we believed in them—but then again, we didn't *not* believe in them. We were easily influenced and very superstitious.

Rumour had it that a certain vacant house in the west end of St. John's was haunted. The house was on Tessier's Lane. Everyone talked about it, but no one was brave enough, or foolish enough, to go in the house and face the consequences. The older boys and girls told us that Old Man Tessier had passed away years before, but that he haunted his house looking for his dead wife, and that he called on the ghosts from the nearby graveyard to protect the house.

One night we were on the corner talking about Tessier's ghost, and one of our friends dared Dickie and me to stay in the haunted house overnight. We took the dare. After all, there was money riding on it, and making money was our one main goal in life.

Tessier's Lane is a small laneway about a quarter of a mile from the General Protestant Cemetery off Old

Topsail Road. The old haunted house is long gone now, but I will never forget the night we stayed there on a dare from Spider Young. He bet us $3 that we wouldn't dare enter Old Man Tessier's house and stay there for two hours or longer. You never backed down on a dare in those days, especially if there was money involved. Dickie and I wanted to be the heroes of Tessier's Lane, and make a dollar or two in the process. We wanted to impress our friends, in particular the young ladies in the group.

It was Halloween night, 1960. Dickie and I huddled under the damp trees across the street from the haunted house. An ominous dark cloud seemed to be sitting on top of the roof of the three-storey dwelling, and wave upon wave of rain was pelting its sides. As we stood in our rain gear surveying the scene, thunder started to roll in the distance. You can guess what was going through our minds, but necessity propelled us forward. It was either face the ghost or drown, or get hit by lightning. Just our luck, the weather staging the event the way it did.

We could not have picked a worse night to go into Old Man Tessier's house. A cat howled in the distance, and Dickie and I suddenly thought that we could see movement behind a second-storey window. Although I knew something Dickie didn't, I still had an eerie feeling about what we were doing. I was afraid Old Man Tessier was going to show up for sure. Dickie asked me if I really thought the house was haunted. I told him it sure looked like it to me. He said that maybe we should give Spider back his money, but I said we had made a bet in front of everyone, and that they would laugh at us if we chickened out. Dickie was shivering, but it was only from the cold; he always had more guts than I did.

The only reason I had agreed to go in Tessier's house was that I had made a plan beforehand. Spider wasn't a bad guy, but he wasn't a close friend, either. I knew Spider didn't believe we would stay in the house, and I guessed he would probably go in there first to make sure we kept up our end of the bargain. Sure enough, another guy squealed on him. He told me that Spider planned to be in there first. So, I got a friend of mine from school, Pete, who wasn't afraid of anything, to hide in the house well before Spider got there. He was supposed to scare the hell out of Spider, who would take off, passing us on the way in. And then we would only have to walk past him and stay in the house for a few minutes to become instant heroes.

As some of our braver friends watched, we approached the house. We were just about to go in when Spider shot past us like a rocket, screaming, "Don't go in there, there's a ghost on top of the stairs!" I knew then that Pete had scared the living daylights out of him. After watching Spider run out of the house, I broke down and told Dickie what had happened. He laughed all the way in the house and up the stairs. We found Pete on the stairway, laughing so hard that we thought he was going to fall over the stairs. He told us how Spider had come creeping up the stairs, scared as hell, while he hugged the wall. Pete had reached out and touched his shoulder, and Spider had freaked out. And then he had said to Spider, in a creepy voice, "You have to come with me to the spirit world."

"The hell I will," Spider said, and took off running.

The three of us sat there laughing for about five more minutes, and then Pete sneaked out the back. Dickie and I stayed for a while, and then we walked out and became the heroes we had imagined we would be. We paid Pete a third of what we got from Spider, and drove Spider nuts about it for years. We never did tell him about the trick we had pulled.

the bully

Every school had its bully, and ours was no exception. Leon Schwartz (definitely not his real name—if I used it and he found out, he would probably beat me up now) was ours, and Dickie and I had many nervous nights wondering if the next day would be our last after a run-in with him. Normally we tried to avoid him, but one year we decided it was time to stop the bullying. It was 1962, and I clearly remember hiding from Leon behind a picket fence one day, thinking, "Please, God, don't let him find me or I'm dead!" I was shaking and sweating, and my heart was pounding so hard I was sure he could hear it, wherever he was. Crouching in the grass, I was sure I didn't have long to live, on account of what I had just done to Leon, which was vandalize his bike.

Leon was the Holy Cross tough guy. He was built like a brick shithouse and he was as tough as nails. Dickie and I had become his favourite targets. We didn't mind facing the rest of the kids in a fight, for we were the devils of Brazil Street, but Leon was forty pounds heavier and a foot taller. Taking on Leon was like taking on five bulldogs—it was committing suicide. Letting the air out of his bike tires had been a way to get even with him, and I was hoping I would get away with it. Even if I didn't, it would be worth the shit-knocking.

I peeked out between the fence posts and couldn't see any movement. I waited a few minutes, then ventured out of hiding. A pair of hands grabbed my shoulders. Concrete Head had me, and I was in deep shit.

"Hey, shrimp, thought you could get away with it, huh?" Leon spun me around.

"Oh, hi, Leon," I said, acting innocent. "I don't know what the hell you're talking about." Visions of being crucified flashed through my mind. When he raised his hands, I waited for the impact, thinking that the beating was worth what I had done to his bike. As he hit me, I thought about getting even with him later. I owed him for more than the beating he was giving me. He had taken my bingo money a few nights before, a whole fifty cents.

When I got home my mom shook her head in exasperation at my soiled and muddy clothes, and asked me what had happened. The white lie, as usual, was ready and waiting, and I delivered it. I told her I had been climbing a fence when it collapsed under me. I apologized for the state of my clothes. She looked at me suspiciously and told me to go upstairs and take a bath. (Many years later she told me she had added up all my little fibs and that there had been enough to fill a 500-page binder! I always thought she believed my fibs. I didn't realize until much later in life how smart parents were.) I didn't like lying to my mom, but I knew that if I told her the truth she would tell Dad, and he would talk to Leon's father, and my revenge, which had already started to percolate in my head, would be ruined.

As soon as supper was finished, I went next door to Dickie's, and we worked on a plan to rid ourselves of Leon's bullying once and for all. It was a thing of promise, but the consequences would be severe if we failed. We decided to lure Leon to Horwood's lumberyard on New Gower Street, and face him. He could beat the crap out of each of us individually, but we knew that the two of us would be a handful for him.

For several days, Dickie and I and some friends started hinting to Leon that the other kids had been meeting secretly about his bullying, and that they were about to go see Brother Angel. We said he should show up at Horwood's lumberyard (the alleged scene of these meetings) to defend his honour. Well, that was enough for him! He bought the story, and told us that Friday would be the last time a group planning to squeal on him would get together. It was a rough week. We were worried that Leon would find out we were lying, and kill us. But he didn't, and that Friday Dickie and I lay in wait in the lumberyard for him. We were afraid, but we knew if we backed down Leon would keep bullying us for the rest of the year.

It was almost dark when we heard Leon approaching the small, makeshift camp we had constructed in the yard. When we were sure that he was within earshot, Dickie began talking to himself in whispers, trying to make it sound as if there were several people inside the structure. Little did Leon know that I was high above him on a wooden frame, waiting to pounce as soon as he started to go inside. Dickie was so convincing that Leon called out to those inside the hut to come out and face him. And then he walked toward the entrance. When he was directly below me, I jumped down on top of him, and then Dickie grabbed him by the feet and dragged him inside. Leon did what all bullies do: he screamed "Unfair!" when he realized that he was outnumbered.

Within minutes we had him on the floor, and he was begging us not to hurt him. We hit him a few times and then told him we'd had enough of his bullying. We said that if he came after either one of us, he was coming after both of us, and we would do worse to him the next time. Leon was speechless, but Dickie put him in a headlock and made him promise he wouldn't bother us anymore.

Half an hour later, we were at Dickie's house celebrating. We jumped, hollered, and laughed. Our troubles with Leon were over—a bully-free year! Hooray!

On Monday morning Dickie and I went to school with a new attitude, after joking all weekend about what had transpired Friday night. We laughed all the way to school. We were still kidding each other about it when Duffy Whelan met up with us a block away from Holy Cross. He asked us if we'd heard what had happened in Horwood's lumberyard on Friday night. We pleaded ignorance while trying to contain our exuberance. Duffy told us it was all over school that six or seven guys had ganged up on Leon Schwartz in the lumberyard, and that he took them down in a huge fist fight that had lasted for nearly an hour. Leon had an idea who two of the attackers were, Duffy said, but he didn't mention it to the police.

Dickie looked at me and we both smiled. Leon had saved face by saying seven guys had roughed him up and he had fought them all off. Big hero. We didn't care, as long as he left us alone. Dickie asked Duffy if Leon had mentioned who the two guys he had recognized were. Duffy looked at us with that thanks-be-to-God-it-wasn't-me look and said no, but Leon's older brother knew and would be looking for them.

That was enough to freeze us in our tracks. Leon's brother was even bigger than he was. We knew then that Leon would have the last laugh, without breaking his promise not to hurt us anymore. His brother was going to do it for him.

And he did. Looking back at it now, though, the roughing-up we got from Leon's brother was nothing compared to the hero's welcome we received from our friends when they found out that we were the brave souls who had tackled Leon in the lumberyard. Leon actually stopped his bullying shortly afterwards, when he realized that the other kids were ready to face him down as well.

This little adventure inspired me with a confidence that would follow me from childhood into adulthood. It made me believe that all obstacles, big or small, could be overcome if approached in the right way with the right person. Of course, my friend Dickie White was that right person. We were just trying to survive in an awkward time in our lives, when growing up was hard enough without the violence. But sometimes fighting was necessary for our self-respect.

Shortly after the encounter with Leon, I was walking home from school one evening when I was approached by two strange boys. One of them asked me if I had any money to give them. I told them to stay away from me or there would be trouble. I can still hear one of them say to the other, "Just look at him. He's got that crazy look in his eyes. He must be from the centre of town." They backed away and left me alone. Ever since that day, I have always felt I could handle any problem or situation. (Dad always told us not to back away from a fight, or show fear, because then that person had you—a bully would never leave you alone if you showed him any fear. It was better to face the guy and get beaten up than to back away from him.) That night I told the guys on the corner what had happened—how two people had backed away from me. Right away, Dickie wanted to know who they were so we could confront them. Good old Dickie, he was afraid of nothing.

the return to tessier's lane

The year after our encounter with the "ghost" on Tessier's Lane, Spider once again gave us the opportunity to be heroes. We were all on the corner one evening when he bought up what had happened in Old Man Tessier's house. He said that he had been the first one in, and that therefore he deserved the glory, not us. The crowd heckled him, so he dared us to go in the house again—another $3 bet—but this time he wanted to go in with us. We accepted Spider's bet.

By this time, the legend of Tessier's ghost had grown to the point where everyone believed that there was a ghost in the house, except, of course, Dickie and me and our buddy Pete. After all, we had been inside the house and we never saw any ghosts, so why should there be one now?

It was during the summer of 1961 that we made a second assault on the ghost of Tessier's Lane. This time we had Spider in tow. He felt safe with us, since we had confronted the ghost the year before and had walked away unscathed. Of course, I had asked Pete to be in the house this time as well, waiting for us and the unsuspecting Spider.

Once inside, Dickie and Spider and I moved around the first floor cautiously. When we had ascertained that the first floor was free of ghosts, we led Spider up to the second floor. Dickie and I could hardly contain ourselves. We walked around the corner and saw movement in the shadows. We froze. There was a figure in the hallway. Spider, thinking that he was seeing the ghost for the second time, started backing toward the stairway.

"You guys do something before it does something to us," Spider said. I shouted to both Spider and Dickie to run down the stairs while I tackled the ghost and saved them. Dickie knew that it was Pete, so he jumped on the "monster" with me. Spider stood there, frozen with fear. I whispered to Pete that he was putting on a great show, and yelled at Spider to run. To his credit, this time he didn't run. He told us to come on, that the ghost had obviously had enough.

With that endorsement, we both jumped off Pete and ran down the stairs and out of the house. A few minutes later we were standing on the other side of the street with some of our friends, who had come to watch us in action. Spider told everyone within earshot how we (himself included) had tackled the ghost. And then he thanked us for what we had done.

While we were talking, I noticed that Pete had shown up, and was gesturing at Dickie and me. I left the crowd and went over to him, and commented on what a marvellous job he had done once again as the ghost of Tessier's Lane—and that we would split the money later. Pete gave me a what-the-hell-are-you-talking-about look and told me he hadn't been in the house. He said he'd had to run an errand for his mother, and hadn't made it on time. I looked at Pete: he was quite serious.

When I told Dickie that it hadn't been Pete, the two of us turned as white as ghosts ourselves. We thought we had possibly fought the real ghost of Tessier's Lane. We actually believed this until a few years later, when Pete confessed that it had been him after all.

A dozen or so years after this, Spider moved to Ontario. Some years later, a relative of his told me that he had died after being in a car accident in 1978. I had often wondered why he stopped writing to us. When I told Dickie the sad news, the first thing he said to me was, "He was a nice guy. I hope that he's found his Orphan Lake."

the catholic boys club

Most of the time we wandered the streets looking for fun. It wasn't until we joined the Catholic Boys Club that we found a more productive way to have fun. The club, situated in a wooden building on St. Clare Avenue (current site of the Knights of Columbus), gave our young lives some stability. Dickie, my brothers, and I joined the club in 1963 or 1964. Nearly all the Catholic boys in the east end were members. Besides the corner boys, Johnny Doyle, Andy Churchill, Jake Jenkins, John Dwyer, and a host of others have said to me that some of the best years of their lives were spent at that club.

The people who ran it were fantastic. Manager Bill Power (a gentler man you could find nowhere) believed that every child should have a chance at being involved in physical fitness and sports. Cecil Joy was the physical fitness instructor, and he took all of us under his wing. Tom "Pussyfoot" Benson, the boxing instructor, had been a light-middleweight champion in one of the amateur fight divisions in St. John's. He also fought several professional fights on the mainland. He was a kind but tough man who hit like a bull when teaching us the ins and outs of boxing. He taught us the finer points of boxing to make us tough in character, not tough in fighting. There was also another gentleman named Tom Mason, who was always there to lend an ear and a hand to anyone who needed a friend to guide them. There were other instructors at the club, but these were the first we had contact with, and they were not only our teachers for many years but friends for life. They were wonderful men who cared about poor kids living in rough neighbourhoods.

There were many activities at the club besides boxing. We became part of the tumbling team, taught by Mr. Joy. We had a floor hockey league that, to us, rivalled the NHL. The teams were always given NHL names. Floor hockey was played with long sticks, and the puck was the rubber covering from the middle of a bowling pin. When you got hit with it—and we wore no padding in those days—it really stung. The only person padded was the goalie. There was always rivalry and pushing and shoving, but win or lose we always left the club at closing time as buddies, and we couldn't wait for the doors to open again the next evening.

We used to play a foolish game on our way home from the club. As we started down Casey Street, we would kick a few doors to get a rise out of the houses' occupants. We did this at least a few times a week, and we didn't hit the same door twice in any given week.

One night, as we were about to kick a door, the owner of the house opened it and threw a bucket of soot from his coal stove right over us. He must have been watching us from behind the curtains. We hightailed it down the street, full of soot and totally ashamed of being so easily surprised. It took about four hours in the bathtub to get the soot off. That was the end of that particular game.

Every year the club held a summer camp in Bay Bulls. It was like entering another world, like a journey to an exotic, faraway land. To the sixty or so of us who went to camp, being fifteen miles from St. John's was the same as being on the mainland.

We played some great jokes on our friends while we were at camp. In those days, Pure Spring and Canada Dry were in opaque green bottles, so it was hard to tell if something besides soda was in them. Some of the boys would put the drinks by their beds, and Dickie and I would open them after they were asleep. We would drink most of the contents, and then fill them back up with vinegar and sugar. And then we would wait for the reaction. When someone woke in the night and took several mouthfuls out of the bottle he had placed by his bed, it usually meant a trip to the river down the lane for a good mouth washing.

Another thing we did was find the backpacks that the others had hidden, and switch the contents—socks, toothpaste, deodorant, shorts, sports shirts, and other items. Most of the boys never noticed until they had put on the wrong clothes or they suddenly tasted a different flavour of toothpaste.

Awards were given out on the Saturday before we went back home from camp. One year, the two camp terrors (us) were each given a pocket knife for being the two best campers. We never figured that one out until many years later, when we asked Cecil Joy why we were even considered for the award: everyone knew that Dickie and I were the ones who played all the practical jokes. Cecil smiled and told us we had made the camp what it was that year with our practical jokes—it "kept everyone loose," he said, and that was what camp was supposed to be all about.

Camp curfew was 10:00 p.m. We were not allowed to leave the campground, but Dickie, Tom Dodd, and I used to sneak out and walk the mile or two down into Bay Bulls to buy stuff at Crane's, the local store, that we couldn't get at the small camp store. The road leading from the camp wasn't lit, and it was very dark and scary. We always scared the daylights out of one another on the way to Bay Bulls, telling ghost stories as we made our illegal trek along that lonely road.

If someone was a bit of a momma's boy, we would, of course, use him for entertainment. This was the case with a boy named Emmanuel (or Emma, as we liked to call him).

The food we had at camp was second to none. We certainly weren't fed like that at home: our parents couldn't afford it. But when we went to the cookhouse for breakfast, three out of four times Emma would stay behind in the bunkhouse. Dickie was always curious about what Emma was doing while the rest of us were eating the breakfast we looked forward to every morning. Dickie said that Emma was up to no good, and one morning when we were on the way to breakfast, he circled back to the bunkhouse. Soon afterwards, he came running to the cookhouse to fetch me. I can still see the big smile on his face. He pulled me away from the table just as I had started eating, and we rushed back to the bunkhouse. Sure enough, Emma was "playing with his britches" when we went in. He jumped out of bed and turned as red as a beet. Dickie smiled at me and then at Emma, and he told Emma that as soon as his mother came to visit him on Sunday he was going to tell her what Emma had been doing. Emma nearly fainted. He begged Dickie not to tell. Dickie said he wouldn't, but only if Emma agreed to do certain things for him and me until camp was over.

We had all sorts of treats for the remaining week of camp. Emma, who was from a well-to-do religious family, shared everything he owned with us, including the cookies his wonderful mom had baked for him, which she brought with her when she came to visit. I often wonder where Emma is now, whether he is alive or dead. He didn't have any contact with us after that—not that I blame him.

where once we roamed

As we grew older and more daring, we broadened our horizons by visiting other parts of St. John's. One day we decided to take a walk to Fort Amherst, on the south side of the harbour, where there was a lighthouse. The first lighthouse on the site was built in 1810. The one that stands there now was built in 1952. Dickie and I had always considered the other side of the harbour as being in another part of the world. Crossing to the south side was a big journey for us. We knew that our parents didn't want us to go too far from home, or to unsafe areas. But kids are always looking for adventure.

One Saturday, we decided to make the trek, without our parents' knowledge. Little did we know that before the day was over, we would go through a door we should not have opened. Some kids at school told us that there was fun to be had at the old fort. Students who lived on Southside Road were always talking about the fort, the Southside Hills, and Freshwater Bay on the other side of the hills. We had it in our minds to go to the south side that Saturday morning, and go we did.

Dickie and Charlie O'Dea and I started on our journey to the fort at about 10:00 a.m. We walked to Southside, where we met up with a few friends from Southside Road. Then we went to the fort. Fort Amherst, opposite Signal Hill, was a military site during World War II. The old battery with its cannon was like a magical kingdom to us. We felt like we were far away from Brazil Street. We explored every nook and cranny. There was an open spot behind the fort, which we decided to jump across—a spot with a drop into the sea about one hundred feet below. Being young and foolish and without fear, we had a fine time jumping across it. And then we decided to walk over the Southside Hills to Freshwater Bay. We didn't realize it at the time, but it was about a four-mile trek. Charlie said that he knew of a path that would take us to a cabin halfway down the slope to Freshwater Bay. We fought our way through the trees for hours, searching for the cabin, before realizing that we were hopelessly lost. But instead of going back, we decided to keep looking for the cabin. Finally, after about five hours, we came upon it. We were very glad to find it. We were so exhausted that, after a small lunch, we lay down and went to sleep. When we awoke it was dark, and well into night. We knew that our parents would be wondering where in the hell we were.

We made a decision, and it was a bad one. We decided to walk back through the woods in the dark to St. John's. It was one of the scariest nights of our young lives. About an hour into our journey, we realized that we should have waited until morning. We had no sense of direction in the pitch blackness. For hours we roamed the Southside Hills, listening to the noises of the forest, which were frightening. We feared that something would jump out of the trees and attack us. At least we still had a good bit of food with us.

Finally, we broke free of the trees. We were on top of the Southside Hills, about a mile from where we had gone into the woods. Finally, we could see the city lights! We figured it was about 9:00, and we knew our parents would be furious with us when we got home. We figured we had been gone about eleven hours. We came down over the hill pretty quickly, headed up the east end of Water Street toward home. Just before we got there, we met a few of the corner boys, who said that our parents had called the police and that everyone was looking for us. Some people thought we had fallen into the harbour and drowned.

It was about 10:00 p.m. by the time we got home. Dickie and I told Charlie that it wouldn't be a good idea to tell our parents we had gone to Freshwater Bay. We made up a story before we reached our houses. When we got home we told our parents—and the police officers—that we had gone to Bowring Park and then on a trek up to the Capsails (a small swimming hole about a mile west of the old park swimming pool), and had gotten lost while exploring the woods in that area. They were so happy to see us that they decided to believe the story, but we were warned never to venture away from home for that length of time again. Another white lie for Mom to add to the 500-page binder!

Charlie, who was from Holyrood, told his grandmother, with whom he was staying in St. John's, that he had been at a friend's house all day. He had lost track of time, he said, and had forgotten to phone. (Luckily, his grandmother and our parents never compared stories, or we would have been killed.) We never did get to see all of Freshwater Bay that day, but the next year we made the same trek, successfully this time. The bay was beautiful. Although we were afraid of going off on our own again, it was well worth it the second time.

Another favourite spot was Signal Hill, where Marconi received the first transatlantic wireless signal in 1901. The little stone building on top of the hill, Cabot Tower, was built between 1897 and 1900, to commemorate Queen Victoria's Diamond Jubilee and John Cabot's voyage to Newfoundland in 1497. Signal Hill is a lovely spot. We spent many days and nights up there looking over the city, especially when it was lit up at night. As children we explored the rocky landscape of the hillside, its trails and caves. When we were older, we practically lived on Signal Hill. If you had a new girlfriend and were serious about her, it wouldn't be a date unless you drove up to the hill for a snuggle.

****

One Sunday, Dickie, Charlie O'Dea, and I decided that we were going to take a bus ride to Holyrood to see where Charlie's parents lived. This time we told our parents where we were going. They seemed to approve. It would get us out of their hair for a full day. What could possibly go wrong, taking a bus to Holyrood, thirty miles away, for one day? Should be no trouble at all, right? But we spent the return fare in Holyrood, and decided to walk back to St. John's. After all, we had walked from Bowring Park many times: what was so hard about walking an extra twenty-odd miles?

We soon found out what was so hard. We left about 2:00 p.m. and walked for about two hours. By that time, we were dropping with exhaustion. It was a very hot day. When we got to Kelligrews, we knew that we had taken on more than we could handle. We had no idea how far we were from St. John's, so we kept on walking. Then we met an old farmer who was heading into the city. He told us that we had walked about twenty miles. Our sunburns proved that we had been out too long. We were nuts to have spent our bus money. We got back in the city at around 9:00 p.m., and this time Dad shouted at us for being so foolish. He said he hoped that we had learned a lesson about spending our money wisely. We told him we had. (At least until our next adventure.)

When we got older, Memorial Stadium became the spot to go to for fun and excitement. We discovered roller skating and, of course, girls: the Stadium was where we could enjoy both. It was the "in" place to go. I would often go down there just for the music alone. The latest hit songs were playing, and many memorable nights were spent trying to pick up the young ladies while the music played.

Wrestling was another highlight for us at the stadium. Some of the great wrestlers of the day—Whipper Billy Watson, Hard Boiled Haggerty, the Great Antonio (who once pulled a city bus by rope several hundred feet as a publicity stunt), the midget wrestlers, and many others—entertained us for hours when we could get tickets to see them. A week without a trip to the stadium was a rare week indeed.

In 1964, the first sod was turned for a shopping mall in St. John's. The Avalon Mall opened in June, 1967, and shopping would never be the same again. (I remember wondering at the time what Mom would have thought of it: she died a month after its doors opened.) The land that the Avalon Mall (called "the mall" to this day, despite the appearance of other malls) was built on had belonged to five brothers and sisters, Jim, Jack, Kathleen, Margaret, and Mary Dillon. Jim and his wife, Joan, had five daughters—Rita, Alana, Geraldine, Ann-Marie, and Judy. I started working for Coca-Cola when the Mall opened, and I dated Alana for a while back then.

Dickie and I practically lived in the area while construction of the mall was going on. It was an enormous project for St. John's, and to me it seemed to be the beginning of a new kind of city. I can still see Premier Joey Smallwood talking proudly about the mall on television, how it would bring new industrial growth to the city. In the early '60s, most of that area was covered by trees. O'Leary Avenue was a dead-end road. Kenmount Road would meet the Trans-Canada Highway in 1965. When the mall opened, industry started to spring up all around its borders. Within a few years, the trees were replaced by businesses.

An area just a stone's throw from the mall became the site of a new hospital. The Health Sciences Complex was officially opened on October 26, 1978, by

Premier Frank Moores. The hospital stands on what used to be called "the sand pits," a popular place for parking (in the romantic sense). You could go in there at any given time and see thirty or forty cars parked, their occupants enjoying the scenery. Dickie and I used to go there often when we started dating girls. It was one of those places the police turned a blind eye to—I guess because half of them were parking there too! When construction started on the Health Sciences, we were sorry to lose our favourite parking area. But the 1960s and 1970s were decades of great growth. Newfoundland was edging its way into the future.

the belmont

One of the most popular drinking establishments in the downtown area was situated across the street from Hogan's Drugstore on Waldegrave Street. The Belmont was a very colourful place. Most of us sipped a few cold ones there at one time or another. I had my first experiences at this tavern at the tender age of twelve, and it would become part of my life for many years. I learned a lot there: it was a stepping stone to growing up.

It is a funny thing about money: when you start to make it after years of having none, you want more. The Belmont and I met as a result of my eternal crusade for money, which I often got by running errands. At the time I was delivering parcels on an old bike for Bob Glasco. One day, as I was making my rounds, I cycled past the Belmont. An inebriated man sitting on the front steps of the tavern asked me if I would ride up the street to Chaulker's and pick him up some food. It was too long a walk for him in his drunken state (about a thousand feet up the road); he said that he would give me twenty-five cents if I ran the errand. Twenty-five cents was nothing to turn up your nose at, and I was happy to make that much for a ten-second ride. The man asked me my name and where I lived, to make sure I wouldn't steal his money. Word soon got around among Belmont patrons that "young Hunt" would, when available, pick up cold and hot food from Chaulker's.

I would go and knock on the door of the club, and a bartender, Hank or Ruby, would go inside and take the orders. I would go to Chaulker's and place them, then take the food back to the Belmont, minus my tips, which on a good day could be $2 to $3. This was an excellent source of extra money every week. Most of my customers were good tippers, thanks to the alcohol. When I was seventeen, I was allowed through the doors of the club. I would talk to the customers and do odd jobs for them, such as walk the women home when the men were too drunk to take them. A lot of the women didn't want to walk alone in that area of town, and they would tip me for accompanying them. I ended up dating a few of their daughters later on down the road, and I still run into some of those ladies today.

A whole new world of opportunity opened up for me. It was very exciting for a kid my age to have access to a bar. The adult world that had eluded me while I stood outside was now unveiled. I was even allowed to have a couple of beers once in a while, because some of the people I did messages for were police officers, and they didn't see anything wrong with a young man having "a beer or two." When they knew that they could trust me (and in our day you did not rip off the police), they became my customers. I even picked up their laundry, brought it back to their cars, and locked it in the trunks—all for a minimal fee, of course.

I also had the pleasure of driving some of the Belmont's patrons home when they were too drunk to drive. (I knew how to drive, but I didn't have a driver's license. In those days you didn't need one to get behind the wheel of a car.) They would pass their keys to me, and I would drive them home. And then I would run back to the Belmont and wait for my next taxi fare. I sometimes drove several people home in the run of a night, and made good money for doing so—they always gave me several dollars each.

If my father had known I was hanging out at the Belmont, he would have killed me. But all he knew was that he never had to give me any spending money. He probably thought I was making enough from my paper route and working for Glasco's. I even lent small amounts of money to my friends, who were obliged to pay it back with interest. A proper little Mafioso, I was.

It was at the Belmont that I got over my prejudice about people from around the bay. The customers there from outside town were the same as we were, very nice people who were perhaps more generous than townies. They treated me like gold during the years I spent at the club.

After a while, I became one of the regulars. Nobody said anything to "young Hunt" because he was protected by the other patrons, particularly the police officers who frequented the club. I felt like I had won the lottery. There was a dog at the Belmont called Two-Four, a name I found odd until I realized he had been named after a case of beer. Every time I went to the Belmont, Two-Four would lie next to me. One evening a drunk guy twice my size started to berate me. He was just about to raise his hand to me when Two-Four growled and jumped at him. The look in Two-Four's eyes was enough to let the guy know that he would come out on the losing end of a scrap with the dog if I were harmed. (I never saw the guy after. I guess one of the cops probably threw him out of the club for good.) Two-Four and I were friends for years. I used to bring him all kinds of scraps from Glasco's. He died after being hit by a truck one day as he ran across the street in front of the Belmont.

One evening I was stopped by two guys (who had obviously been drinking), outside the club, and they asked me if I had any cigarettes or money to give them. I had money, since I was just coming back from Chaulker's with an order for one of the off-duty police officers who happened to be inside the club having a few cold ones. I also had cigarettes, but I told them both that I worked hard for my cigarettes and I wasn't about to give them away. "Go to hell," I said. They decided to try to prevent me from getting into the club, but one of the customers who was leaving saw what was happening and went inside to get Harold, the police officer for whom I was doing an errand. I had his lunch in my hand. One guy made the mistake of pushing me to the ground, slipping part of Harold's lunch into his mouth and then reaching his hand inside my jacket pocket for my cigarettes. The poor guy never knew what hit him. Harold grabbed him from behind, and another police officer put the guy who was with him in a headlock. They wrestled both the guys to the ground. Then the cops roughed them up, put the cuffs on, and attached them to a telephone pole. Harold told Ruby to phone "the boys" and tell them to send the Black Maria for two men who had assaulted a young man in front of the Belmont. Harold told me that after they had a few beers they would visit Fort Townshend and give the guys a little "talking to" for putting their hands on me. That meant a beating was in store for them.

Life was great. Not only was I allowed in the Belmont, but I had some of St. John's finest on my side. I often wondered what happened to the two guys who tried to take my cigarettes.

Just a few months before this, it was a different story with another police officer. Dickie and I had "borrowed" some cigarettes from Kenney's Fruit Store, a few doors away from the Belmont. I remember that they were Rothmans ("Rockmans" to Dickie), a favourite cigarette of the day. We were cleaning out the storage area at the back of the store for Mr. Kenney, and when we finished he gave us some money. When we got outside, Dickie dragged me into a laneway and showed me five packs of cigarettes he said he had found in a box. They couldn't belong to Mr. Kenney, he said. He had found the box outside the back entrance. (My guess was that he had found it inside and had taken it outside, but who was I to contradict a friend?)

We were in a laneway puffing away when a police officer appeared. To this day, I can still see his face. He asked us what we were doing there. We tried to conceal the cigarettes, but we weren't quick enough. "Where did you guys get these cigarettes?" he asked. Caught by surprise, we instinctively lied. (But we were shaking in our boots: fear of the police was huge in those days, and this was the first time we had lied to a police officer.) We told him we had just found the cigarettes, and that we had been about to call the police and report our discovery. He looked at us very suspiciously and said that cigarettes had been stolen from a business on Water Street a few days ago, and that these might be part of the haul from the robbery. Now we were really scared: not only had we taken the cigarettes from Kenney's, but we had somehow become implicated in a burglary. The cop looked at me and Dickie. He knew he had scared the crap out of us. Dickie and I both blurted out together, "We don't know anything about any robbery, officer." He told us he was going to have to confiscate the cigarettes, but he wouldn't tell our parents if we kept quiet about the whole business. If we agreed, he would let us off with a warning, he said.

Well, he didn't have to tell us twice. We both agreed readily. After all, a police officer would never lie to us, right? I can still see him walking up New Gower Street, smoking away at the cigarettes that he had confiscated. I can remember that moment in my mind as if it were frozen in time, right down to the sun shining on our faces. Dickie and I stared at his back. "Prick," said Dickie. I had to agree. "That rotten, lousy bastard, Dickie. I hope he chokes on our smokes." We learned a valuable lesson that evening. Trust no one, ever, not even the police.

I ran errands for the Belmont for a while. Then

there more interesting things to concern myself with in my teenage years, such as finishing school, finding work, and discovering girls. (Not necessarily in that order.) Work came sooner than I thought: I landed my first full-time job at seventeen. It was with my dad at CN, and it gave me my first taste of what adult life was like.

cn: a new world opens

After I graduated from Brother Rice in 1966, I had to decide what I wanted to do with my life. Dickie and I and a friend of ours, Tom Dodd, decided to go into the army. But Mom and Mrs. White didn't want Dickie and me to be sent to some place in the world where there was unrest (at that time the Canadian military was sending peacekeeping forces to Cyprus, where there was civil war), so Dickie and I stayed behind in St. John's while Tom enlisted in the army. After his training, Tom was sent to Cyprus, and returned unscathed. He spent twenty-five years in the military, with The Black Watch, and later on, he ended up being my boss from 1999 to 2009, when I was with The Canadian Corps of Commissionaires.

When I went to bed at night as a young child, I used to listen for the sound of the passenger train as it left the station. Or the freight train as it hauled supplies to other parts of the province. I remember thinking that one day I would work on the trains. In those days, it was glamorous to be associated with the Canadian

National Railway. And my childhood dream came true—for a while, at least—I joined my father and my brother as an employee of CN. You had to be at least nineteen to be hired by CN, but Dad pulled some strings. And so I found myself on the Newfie Bullet—the nickname of the *Caribou*—an oxymoron if there ever was one. The Bullet took approximately twenty-four hours to make the trip between St. John's and Port aux Basques, a distance of 571 miles.

In my forty-five years of working, the year and a half that I spent with my father at CN was the hardest job I ever had. The money was fantastic for those days, but you really earned it. My brother Edward had started the year before I did, when he finished school at Holy Cross. We never did work together, though, as we were on opposite shifts. I was on the 101, and he was on the 102.

Working for CN Railway brought me from childhood to manhood, and I was schooled by the nicest group of people I have ever encountered in my life. Perhaps I was treated so well—as one of the boys—because of the respect they had for my father. As soon as I began working with Dad, I could tell he was well-liked and well-respected by his co-workers. He was sociable with everyone, and always there to help anybody who needed a hand. I ended up working with the same dedication, and people often said to Dad, about me, "like father, like son."

I became closer to my father during the trips we made together. (Of course, I was an angel when he was on board, but reverted to being less angelic when he wasn't.) I always followed his example when he was there. He had a charm about him at work that I never saw displayed at home, a certain flair that attracted people to him like a magnet. His kindness to others made me proud to be his son, and I often wished I was more like him. My brother Ed has often said that Dad would never die as long as I'm alive. I have a lot of his mannerisms.

I will never forget my first trip. I went on the 101 a greenhorn and came back seasoned three days later, in politeness especially. Even though the hours were long and the work was difficult, I couldn't wait to go back out again.

The 101 left St. John's about 1:00 p.m. and got into Port aux Basques the next night around the same time. This was because of all the stops it had to make in the towns and junctions it passed through. On the way to the west coast we always made a stop near Corner Brook at a place called Cook's Brook, where the 102 (usually with Ed on board) would pass the 101 on its way back to St. John's. We would stay there for about an hour. The trains also made unscheduled stops when they struck a moose or a cow. Local people would come and help the railway workers remove the animal. I guess the families who helped out shared the carcass. Nothing was wasted in those days.

On my first day of work, I went to the main terminal and waited for nearly an hour for someone to come and take me to the train. It was about 8:00 p.m. Dad was a stickler for being at work on time. When the terminal worker arrived, he and I walked out through the back to the train, which was parked about ten feet behind the building. This made it easy for people who were handicapped to board the train, the worker told me. It was starting to get dark as I entered my new world. When I stepped onto the platform and boarded the 101, I could feel my life changing.

We had to be at work by 9:30 p.m., to prepare for the long trip across the island the next day. I boarded at 9:00 sharp, to impress my new bosses. I was taken to the coach next to where the passengers and crew ate, and shown how to carry out the duties of my job, which was dishwasher. I decided that the job was not going to be too bad after all. Was I ever wrong!

At 11:00 p.m., all hands turned in to bed. I can still remember the train getting ready to pull out of its berth in St. John's, and the wonderful anticipation of adventure as it finally pulled away from the railway yard on Water Street. I soon fell asleep to the motion of the train moving along the tracks and the clanging of the steel wheels.

Before I knew it, I was being called out of my bunk to start my day in the pantry, where I was to wash dishes for the 142 people who had boarded in St. John's or whom we had picked up along the route while I was sleeping. The day started at 5:30 a.m. Breakfast began at 6:00. I was taking it easy when the first load of dishes found their way in. A half-hour later, as people finished their meal, an avalanche of dishes and cutlery started, the likes of which I had never seen before. I didn't stop washing until around 10:00 a.m. Some days I would be washing until 10:30. Then there was just time for a short rest until dinner started at noon. It took us until 3:00 or 4:00 to clean up the dinner mess. Then we got another hour-long break, and we were back at it again for supper at 5:00, finishing up by 9:00 p.m.—if we were lucky.

By the time the day ended, you were so tired that you fell into bed after a quick wash. I remember thinking that first night, "What did I let Dad get me into?" But, even so, I realized I was very lucky to have a job when so many others were out of work. There was no backing out. I resigned myself to my lot, which became easier as time went on, and I got used to it. (Just keeping steady on my feet was difficult at first. Anyone who has walked inside a train knows that it's not always easy to keep your balance. But after a few trips, my body adjusted itself, and going down the aisles became as easy as walking down a city street.)

I met Shannon Coombs after my second trip, and he treated me like a younger brother. He was maybe five or six years older than I was, at peace with himself and the world. Shannon was very easygoing and honest. He introduced me to the ladies who used the trains for business travel; there were local women, and women from Montreal, Toronto, and other places on the mainland. He taught me how to play cards, how to stay up half the night having a few drinks, and how to be ready for work at 6:00 in the morning. Being young and naive helped me tremendously. I followed his every move. He became my mentor. By the sixth or seventh trip, I was a seasoned veteran who could play cards, have a few beers, and talk to the ladies with the best of them!

Shannon warned me about a "Mr. Cook," who was "different." When I asked him why, he just shook his head and told me to avoid him. Dad told me the same thing about Mr. Cook, and that if he ever bothered or touched me to let him know and he would take care of it. With Dad on side, I had no worries about Mr. Cook, but I still wondered why everyone was so wary of him, so damn naive was I at that age. On my eighth trip, I found out why.

I was in the pantry cleaning up a bunch of dishes one evening after supper, when in came Mr. Cook. He started talking up a storm. We were in deep conversation when he moved closer to me, which made me feel uncomfortable, as did the way he looked at me. He leaned on the counter with his hands folded across his chest, waiting for me to reply to a question he had asked. I can't remember the question, but it had sexual overtones. I decided to tell Mr. Cook my name, and it was as if he had been struck by lightning. He asked me if I was Ned Hunt's son. When I said yes, he apologized and said that he had only been joking, and asked me not to tell my father about the conversation. But I did tell my father. His only words were, "Don't you worry, Robert, I'll take care of it. You just go to work on next Tuesday."

I didn't see Mr. Cook again. When I asked Shannon where he was, he grinned and told me that my father had taken care of Mr. Cook. I found out about a month later from an old-timer working on the train that Dad had convinced Mr. Cook he would be better off working in the terminal warehouse than on the 101 or 102, especially if he ever went near one of his sons again.

I loved the nights when we sat down to talk or to have a game of 120s after supper. The food that was served on the Bullet was the best, and there was always a big feed of leftovers for us to have with a couple of beers. Although the work was exceptionally hard, it was one of the best times of my life. There was great camaraderie among the men, which they extended to me. I was accepted as one of them, and forty-three years later I still appreciate their generosity. The people who worked with CN seemed to like their jobs, and I never saw one of them being rude to a customer. In those days there were no women working on the trains, but they did work in the main office in the terminal. They were treated with the greatest of respect; it was always "Yes, ma'am" or "No, ma'am" when they asked us a question.

As I mentioned, everyone had respect for Dad. One evening, a certain person who worked in the terminal got angry with me when I put a box on the train without permission. He started yelling that I was not to put anything aboard without his say-so. And then he asked me my name. When I told him I was Ned Hunt's son, he said I should have let him know who I was. He never bothered me again.

Once, I was asked to join in a game of poker with some of the regular passengers and a few of the crew members. I often heard Dad say that I should be careful about playing such games, because I could lose a lot of money. I asked Shannon's advice, and he told me to get into the game. He said he would keep an eye on me, and let me know if it was getting too heavy. I was lucky that night: I won about $40. But when Dad heard about my gambling, he put a stop to it. He said that some people would let you win to keep you coming back to the game, and then they would take you for all you were worth. I never played poker again after his warning. I stuck to crib and growl with Shannon and a few of the others.

A part of my job was deciding on the breakfast size, whether it would be continental or full-meal. How far the train was from St. John's determined whether there would be a full breakfast of bacon, bologna, eggs, and cereal or just a light one of tea or coffee, toast, and juice. The distance to town was on mileage markers attached to the telephone poles on the side of the tracks, each a mile apart. If we were more than fifty miles from St. John's, a full breakfast was served. If not, only a light breakfast. Of course, we always hoped we were fewer than fifty miles from home, because a full breakfast would take longer to clean up. We would have to stay behind to finish this chore when we got into the city. Or perhaps not. We used to throw dishes out the window and into the woods if we were about fifteen miles from town, because we knew we wouldn't be able to finish cleaning them all before we arrived. If you were to walk the old railway bed and explore the adjacent woods, you might still find some old CN dinner plates, cups, saucers, knives, forks, and spoons. We must have cost CN a fortune in dishes and cutlery!

After dinner, individually wrapped peppermints were given to the passengers. As we went through Bowring Park on our way home, we would throw them over the wire fence to the kids. The kids loved it. The train would always slow down going through the park, and crowds always gathered to see the Bullet passing by. It was a highlight of the trip for us. After a few runs, I became an expert at tossing the mints, hardly ever missing the fenceline.

I made several trips on the Bullet when Joey Smallwood was on board. Smallwood always travelled with an entourage, and usually had a coach to himself. When you served Smallwood and his colleagues lunch or brought drinks to their meeting room, you had to do so very quietly. It used to fascinate me, knowing that these men were running the province from the train. Being a pantry boy, I rarely got the chance to enter their coach. But once, Shannon, the serving waiter of that particular night, allowed me to take them their drinks and their lunch. As I mentioned, it took a while to learn how to walk through the coach while the train was moving. You had to be especially careful of your balance when you were carrying drinks and food. Thinking about this had made me really nervous, since I was about to serve the premier of the province—so nervous that, when I knocked on the coach door, I did so loudly and aggressively. The gentleman who opened the door was about to say something to me, when Mr. Smallwood asked me my name. I told him, then apologized for the noise I had made. He replied, very kindly and gently, that the next time I served them, I should knock on the door without breaking it down. I nodded and said, "Yes, sir," and they all laughed. I laughed along with them. Smallwood then told one of his associates to give me a tip, and I hurriedly put it in my pocket and rushed away. When I left the coach I looked at it—it was a $5 bill! That was a very big tip in those days. The average tip was between twenty-five and fifty cents. Of course, I gave it to Shannon when I got back. It was his shift, and therefore the money was rightfully his. But, being a good guy, he split it right down the middle with me.

I made $144 every two weeks. That was a huge amount of money for a young man back then, when the average working salary was anywhere from $50 to $100 a week. CN always paid its employees well. I was on cloud nine when I got my first pay envelope. I gave Dad $40 for board. In those days, once you started to work you had to pay board and help with the bills. (Try that on today's kids!) I was on top of the world, getting paid a man's salary. Surely I had found my Orphan Lake, and I hoped that Dickie would soon find his. (And so he did, when he went to work for St. John's city council a short time later.)

I took Dickie out to lunch on my first payday, which cost about $8 for both of us. We went to Bowring's and had a huge meal, with dessert. Then I went on a shopping spree, buying new pants, shoes, shirts, sweaters, and my first watch. These were things that I could never have afforded before. I must have spent $50 on clothes and lunch, an unheard-of sum in my life. That night, I took the girl I was dating to The Pioneer restaurant on Portugal Cove Road.

Many people used the railway in those days. I met nurses, salesmen, and government employees, and police officers who were picking up prisoners from different parts of the island and transferring them to the lockup or the penitentiary in St. John's. It was at this time that the ladies really started to catch my eye. Many a lass travelled on the rails to get to work. I met a young lady one evening who was going back to St. John's after visiting her aunt in Corner Brook. Her name was Amanda Tucker, and I dated her for two months before she went away to the mainland.

I was having all kinds of new experiences in those days. I remember Dad saying to me that all things come in due time, and not to be too anxious to grow up. But I was into a whole new learning stage, and I couldn't get enough of it.

As I was getting things sorted out in the diner one night, Shannon told me that on our return trip we were going to have a really tough prisoner, Bruiser Malone, on board. There were going to be police officers coming from St. John's to pick up this guy in Corner Brook. He was a notorious criminal and a very dangerous person, Shannon said.

Two police officers spoke to me at great length that night about Bruiser Malone. They told me that he was a mobster, whom their counterparts in Corner Brook had apprehended when he was trying to sneak out of Newfoundland and back to the mainland. They said that he had killed two men in Montreal in a mob hit, and they were taking him to St. John's to stand trial. He would definitely be sentenced to life, they said, and sent to a prison in Ontario to serve his sentence. We all had to be very careful of him when he came on board, they told me, even though he would be in handcuffs. I had never seen a real crook, and I was excited (and a bit worried) about having the opportunity to do so.

The officers got off the 101 in Corner Brook; I remember them telling the porter on the way out that they would be back when they had picked up their prisoner, and to make sure the coach they were going to ride in was empty. I spent the rest of the trip wondering what the prisoner looked like. I drove Shannon nuts talking about it. The hours flew by. We went to Port aux

Basques and returned to Corner Brook, picking up the police officers and their prisoner. They entered the last coach, next to the caboose, and I figured that the brief glimpse I had of them would be my only sighting. And then Shannon told me that one of the officers had requested that I bring them their lunch. Naturally, I said that he must be kidding. When I found out he wasn't, I decided that I was going to show the boys that I had guts—no prisoner could frighten me!

Shannon had gotten the food trays ready for me, and I took them to the prisoner's coach and knocked on the door. It opened, and one of the police officers asked me to step inside. I looked at the cuffed gangster, and he eyed me as I laid the food down on the berth. I had just finished, when he said that he knew me from somewhere. I replied that I didn't know him. But he pointed at me and told the two police officers that someone had told him I had done a theft in St. John's only two months before, and that I must be hiding out with CN to avoid capture. I was shocked! I looked at him and said that he must be mistaken. I wasn't a thief. Then it occurred to my small brain that maybe some of the things that Dickie and I had done years before had caught up to me. I was just about to confess all—how Dickie and I had "borrowed" things over the years—when the three of them burst into laughter. Little did I know that Shannon and the others were also laughing their heads off outside the coach.

The "gangster" was actually another police officer, who had been in Corner Brook on business. They had concocted the story to have a laugh at my expense. I started laughing when Shannon and the others came into the coach. I laughed so much that I nearly cried. I'd been had, and well had. I told the story of that practical joke on many trips between Port aux Basques and St. John's.

In 1968, CN introduced the trans-island Road Cruiser bus service, and the following summer full passenger service by train was discontinued. Some mixed service (passenger and freight) survived until 1988. Most of the rails were pulled up and scrapped by 1990. My job with CN ended in 1967, when I went to went to work for Coca-Cola, where I would remain for the next twenty-five years. Edward finished with them the following year, and Dad in 1969.

The trains are gone now, but the sound of the whistle still echoes in my ears every time I go into Bowring Park. The short time I spent working on them changed my life forever. It gave me a sense of direction and a solid introduction to working life. The people I worked with were hard-working and true and had a wonderful attitude toward life.

time moves on

Dickie and I didn't see much of each other in the next few years. His job and mine and dating the ladies kept us apart. We had met new friends, and we got together only once in a while, to go to dances or clubs.

One night we were at the Silver Stallion on Brookfield Road. There were three of us, Dickie and me and Vic Walsh, a guy who worked with me at Coca-Cola. I had just gotten my first car, a dark green Pontiac, from Terra Nova Motors, behind the old Newfoundland Hotel at the time. The car was only a year old, and a beauty. It had cost me $700, taxes in.

When we left the club and got back in the car, Dickie and I started clowning around, and Vic began egging us on to fight each other. We had been acting like idiots all night, mostly on account of the alcohol. Dickie was sitting in the front seat, and he was really getting on my nerves. He kept turning the steering wheel, and I would have to drive in whatever direction the car was pointing. After about ten rounds of this, I'd had enough. To Vic's glee, I told Dickie to stop or I would pull the car over and call him outside. I can still see the look on Dickie's and Vic's faces: they thought I was nuts. After all, Dickie was about seventy-five pounds heavier than I was. But Dickie kept it up, and I finally stopped the car, on Smith Avenue. I was as mad as hell, and called both Dickie and Vic outside.

For the first time since we had met, I found myself pitted against my friend, and there was no backing out. That thing called honour had to be upheld. The next few minutes were a bit of a blur. I pushed Dickie, and he picked me up with one hand. I ended up in the grass on the other side of a fence. Vic suddenly went silent. He knew that we had crossed the line. I couldn't believe what had happened in a moment of anger.

I climbed back over the fence, got into my car, and drove home. The next day, not a word was said about the incident. Dickie and I resumed our friendship as if nothing had happened. Not a bad word had ever passed between us before that night, and the same held true afterwards.

****

It was around this time that we corner crowd got some new additions to our family. One night in the early '70s, while we were on the corner shooting the breeze, we met some guys from Quidi Vidi—"the Gut." Paul, Jack, Walter, and Skeets Barrington were their names. Paul and Jack became regulars, and they spent many afternoons and nights with us, roaming the city in search of fun.

Late one night, about twenty of us went to Bannerman Park, and at 1:00 a.m. we jumped over the fence. We had decided to go for a swim in the park pool. We were in the pool for about an hour and having ourselves a very entertaining time (we had taken plenty of beer with us), when we heard sirens. We scrambled, half dressed, while about ten police officers tried to catch us. The police were in hot pursuit. One of them shouted at us to stop or he would shoot, but we kept on going—the police didn't carry guns in those days. It was a comedy of errors, a real farce, and not one of us got caught.

About an hour later, several of us were standing on the corner having a great laugh about it all when a police cruiser pulled up and the officer asked us if we had seen a bunch of guys go by. The cop described them to us, and we told him that we had seen them earlier and that they had said they were heading to Victoria Park to jump the fence and go swimming. The cruiser drove off with a screech of tires. We had another great laugh at that. We were always trying to get even with the police, because they often got in the way of our nighttime fun.

This kind of fun was soon to become a thing of the past. In a few short years I met my wife and moved to another area of St. John's, leaving behind my youthful, carefree days. They say that the only things you can't control in life are death and taxes, but there's a third thing: time. It moves on, and we can never stop it or predict what it has in store for us.

Dickie and I started to drift apart as we got older and our work commitments began to increase. Gone were the days when he and I would stroll downtown looking for fun and adventure. But a whole world of new adventures was open to us, because now we had something we had never been accustomed to: money. For the next five or six years, Dickie and I enjoyed the things that we had dreamed of as kids growing up in the centre of the city. We also had girlfriends. (I was seeing Rita Powell and Dickie was dating Sheila Forristall, both of whom lived on McKay Street.) Life was pretty good. Orphan Lake was finally becoming a reality for us. Life was finally starting to look up. The shadows of the past were dissolving and we were on our way.

Then fate reared its ugly head. In the fall of 1973, Dickie was involved in a traffic accident. He and two of his co-workers, Mike Beard and Anthony Murphy, were driving a council truck that had just left the garage after repairs. They were going down Viking Road when the front wheels fell off the truck and it rolled over. Mike and Anthony were able to get out, but Dickie was trapped inside. It took paramedics and firefighters several hours to free him from the wreckage.

Dickie, my best friend and mentor, was never the same afterwards. He had sustained a severe back injury, from which he never fully recovered. The accident followed him for the rest of his life. He never went back to work, and he never married.

In 1971 I met my wife, Sharon. We were married in 1976. I moved from Brazil Street and began a new journey.

Now I'm sixty-two. As I look back at my life, I realize I had it pretty good compared to others of my era. Growing up on Brazil Street in the '60s and '70s wasn't easy, but it did instill values and morals. Friends and family moulded us into what we are today: they taught us the value of hard work and how to approach it and everything else in a positive way. They showed us how to have fun. Above all, they taught us respect for other people, something that seems to be lacking in today's youth.

I would like to think that Dickie has finally found his true Orphan Lake. I know I will too, some day. Perhaps I'll meet him there. Maybe there will even be a Brazil Street, a Paramount Theatre, and a Bowring Park. Who knows? I know that family members and friends who have passed on will be there, and we will be together once again. Dickie and the rest of us will stand on that same corner, swapping stories and the secrets of life. That is my hope.

acknowledgements

I would like to thank the people at Flanker Press who made the publication of this, my first solo book, possible. They include owners Garry, Margo, and Jerry Cranford, and the other wonderful people of Flanker who have been so helpful to me: Bob Woodworth, Laura Cameron, Jennifer Best, and Peter Hanes. And a very special thanks to Dwayne LaFitte, who gave Lisa Ivany and me our writing break in 2004, when he okayed our first book, *Christmas Memories*. Thank you, Dwayne, for offering the world of writing to us both. You are a special person.

Special thanks also go to the many people who have read my work and offered positive comments, particularly Beulah Parsons-Paddle, Judy Cranford, Edwina Kenny, Carl Morton, Steve White, Noreen and Bob Janes, Elaine Hiscock, Terri Farrell, and my brothers Edward, Calvin, Hubert, and Angus.

A sincere thanks to that wonderful person in my life, Marion Penney, a special lady who has read this book several times. Your inspiration, understanding, and love changed the course of many parts of it, making it truly more readable.

I would be remiss if I didn't extend a special thanks to Janice Brien for her excellent editing work. Also, I wish to thank former teacher Mike Kelly for answering many of the questions that required his knowledge and wisdom.

Thanks go out to my sister-in-law Virginia Hunt for her information on the Health Sciences Complex. Many thanks also to Jane Eales and Melanie McLeod of the Bowring Park Foundation.

Special thanks to Neachel Keeping of the City of St. John's for her information on the Newfoundland Railway. Also thanks to Helen Miller, City of St. John's archivist, for her help in locating some of the photos. I also wish to thank Susan Rendell for her superb editing. Her unique insight has been invaluable.

Thank you, Stephen and Heather. And a special thanks to Sharon.

A great deal of thanks is owed to all the corner boys and girls for being the beautiful people they were and still are. They made the writing of this book possible.

Robert Hunt was born and raised in St. John's, where he still lives. He is the father of two children, Stephen and Heather. Robert's other books include *Christmas Memories*, *At Heart*, and *Christmas Treasures*, all co-written with Lisa J. Ivany. He can be reached by email at bobhunt99@yahoo.ca.